ALSO BY BRUCE CLEMENTS

Two Against the Tide
The Face of Abraham Candle
From Ice Set Free
I Tell a Lie Every So Often
Coming Home to a Place You've Never Been Before
with Hanna Clements
Prison Window, Jerusalem Blue
Anywhere Else but Here
Coming About
Tom Loves Anna Loves Tom

The Treasure of Plunderell Manor

The Treasure of Plunderell Manor

Bruce Clements

A Sunburst Book
Farrar, Straus & Giroux

Library of Congress catalog card number: 87-25218
Published in Canada
*by HarperCollins*CanadaLtd
Printed in the United States of America
First edition, 1987
Sunburst edition, 1991

For Pablo and Jeff,

two very special characters

The Treasure of Plunderell Manor

1

LAUREL BYBANK WAS WALKING fast along the road to Plunderell Manor. The sky was gray, a cold wind was blowing against her back, and she was feeling tired. All day yesterday she had walked in the rain. Today the mud in the road was frozen solid, and the ice around the hem of her dress clicked as it hit the tops of her shoes.

She had been on the road for five days. Five days of buying food through kitchen doors, because nice girls didn't go to inns alone, five days of looking for friendly people who would let her have part of a bed, or a dry place in the barn, for a penny, or for nothing, five days of being hungry most of the time and sleeping in wet clothes, five days of not having a place to call her own.

She pulled her cloak tighter around herself and started walking faster. The road turned right and curved down through a hemlock forest for about a quarter of a mile and then came out into the open again and ran in a straight line between two meadows. In the meadow to the left were two black horses, their legs and stomachs splattered with mud. They stood next to each other, almost touching, and watched her. The bigger one lifted his nose into the air and smelled for snow, but he kept his eye on her.

She jumped across the narrow ditch next to the road and went to the hedge. "Good day. Would you care to visit? You're very beautiful."

They didn't move.

"I wish I had a pocket full of apples, or pears, or a bit of sugar, but I don't. Next time, I promise."

She reached toward them and opened her hand. The bigger horse stepped back and spun around and started to move away, and the other one followed. In a few seconds they were trotting toward the far corner of the field, blowing steam behind them. They stopped under a tree and looked at her again.

"Next time," she said quietly, "I really will bring you something, and we'll set off being friends."

She jumped back onto the road and started walking again. She loved horses. She had a scar across her left knee from the time Sweet Ben, Father Simpson's horse, had knocked her down and bitten her. But Ben had been very young then, and so had she, and he hadn't meant her any harm. Horses were better than most people. They had purer souls, she was sure of that, even though they weren't supposed to have souls at all. She liked feeding them, hitching them up, driving them night or day, brushing them, and talking to them. She even liked the way they smelled. She had looked after cows, too, and most of them were quite nice, but it was hard to be friends with a cow.

A big snowflake drifted down in front of her, slowly

turning over and over until it hit the ground. She shifted her satchel from her left shoulder to her right. It wasn't very heavy, but the strap was narrow and it cut into her. Her stomach gurgled. "It won't be long now," she said. "The kitchen at Plunderell Manor is absolutely bound to be as big as a house. A whole wall of food. Bread. Raisins. Fish directly from the river. Butter and cheese. Endless."

She thought about Father Simpson and the rectory at St. Anne's Church, where she had lived and worked for the last six years. Father Simpson had always talked about whole walls of things. He would come into the kitchen and tell her he was going to drink a whole wall of ale, or he would ask for his cassock and say that he was going across to the church to hear the confessions of a whole wall of sinners, or he would take her hand at night when she was reading to him and say she was as good as a whole wall of saints, and that he would have died ten times over without her there to take care of him.

And now, after a long, final illness, he was dead. He had made the Great Change. God had taken him out of this hard life. He was up in heaven, surrounded by walls and walls of angels, remembering her and watching over her and expecting her to do the right thing. She looked up at the sky. "I'll do what you told me as best I can. Truly I will. I know you don't want me to cry, but I miss you. It's very selfish. I'll try to be better."

She wiped her eyes with the back of her hand and kept looking up at the sky. It was too cloudy to see where the sun was, but she knew it wasn't late in the day. She had passed the Saltfield railway station at noon by the station clock, and a woman sweeping the steps had told her it was less than ten miles to the old stone bridge down the hill from the manor. She could walk ten miles in three hours, so it wasn't yet three o'clock, and she didn't have to worry. The main thing when you were traveling was not to find yourself alone on the road at night. You had to plan ahead and keep your eyes open. "God takes care of careful girls," Father Simpson had said to her a thousand times, and she knew it was true.

She reached under her cloak, undid the top two buttons on her dress, and felt for her money pouch. She wasn't really worried about losing it, since it had a new leather thong, but it didn't do any harm to make sure it was still there. Father Simpson had given it to her the day before he died, gripping her hand very tightly and making her promise never to take it off, especially when she was traveling or living among strangers. There were seven shillings and three pennies in it, plus her flint and steel and her colored chalks. She counted the coins through the soft leather and tugged on the thong to make sure the knot at the back of her neck was still tight, and then she buttoned her dress again.

Seven shillings was a lot of money. Robbers had killed people for less than seven shillings, or knocked them on the head and left them in the ditch for dead. It was a dangerous world. Still, as Granny Piersall had told her when she was very little, if you did your work, and knew your place, and trusted God, nobody in the world could harm your soul. "And it helps to be sommat ugly," she had said. "Not ugly enough to put the hens off laying, just enough to make the wrong men pass you by. And have a clean face and hands. Dirt draws dirt."

Laurel wondered, sometimes, if Granny had been telling her that she was ugly, but she never asked, knowing it would be a vanity. She stopped near a little pool in a table rock and wet her hands and face and dried them on her neck cloth. "I mustn't forget the two horses," she said out loud. "My first errand to Saltfield, I must remember to bring apples. They're bound to have an apple barrel in the kitchen."

The road led into a thick woods. She heard a wagon coming behind her. She didn't turn around, but when it got close she stepped to the side between two big trees and let it roll by. There were two men in it, one old and tall and thin, the other small and hunched over, with a face like a squirrel. The old man slowed the wagon down, perhaps to offer her a ride, but the squirrel-faced man poked him in the ribs and he speeded up again and they drove by.

As she was stepping back onto the road, she looked into the woods and saw someone moving. She pretended not to notice, and started walking fast, keeping him in sight out of the corner of her eye. As the road started to climb, he disappeared. Halfway up the hill, she decided that if she could see the end of the woods when she got to the top, she would pick up the front of her skirt and start running, taking advantage of the slope to speed her up. She said a prayer of thanksgiving for God's protection, took some deep breaths, and felt calmer.

Just as she was reaching the top of the hill, a young

man stepped out onto the road in front of her. He was about eighteen years old, tall, with dark brown eyes and a narrow nose and a small scar on his chin. "Good day," he said. "No need to be afraid. John Frame, steward, at your service. You're looking for Plunderell Manor, are you not?"

Laurel took a step back. A stick cracked under her foot, and she jumped. Her heart was pounding.

He smiled. "That is where you're going, isn't it, if I may ask? Plunderell Manor?"

Laurel took a deep breath. "I must be on my way."

"You're Mistress Alice Plunderell's new maidservant, Laurel Bybank. I've been watching for you ever since Lord Stayne sent his letter to the Bishop. I never minded it. It's part of a steward's job, seeing after the servants."

Laurel drew a cross on the ground with her foot. "I don't mean to be rude. I wish I could stand and chat, but truly I can't."

"Rude? No. Last thing." He stepped to the side of the road. "I've made you afraid. I'm sorry."

She shook her head. "No, you haven't. Well, yes, you have."

"Please, go along if you need, but there's no hurry. You're not two hundred yards from the river. You can hear it if you turn your ear that way. Once you're across the bridge, Plunderell's directly in front of you at the top of the hill. Ugly place. It's home to me, and I don't mind a bit the way it looks, but you have to be honest with honest people, don't you? And ugly is ugly. Do you know anything about the manor?"

"They're keeping a place for me."

"Is that all you know?"

"I don't need to know any more now."

"Not so, Laurel Bybank. The more you know, the safer. May I tell you something else? It's in your interest. Everyone's really."

"Yes, I suppose."

"They want Mistress Alice dead. Lord and Lady Stayne. Nothing less will satisfy them."

Laurel bit her lower lip. She had been taught never to listen to people telling stories about other people. Still, she wanted him to go on.

"Mistress Alice will be eighteen a week from today," he said. "She will then be Lady Alice, Mistress of Plunderell. If she dies before then, it's all theirs, including the hidden treasure. Do you believe in progress in everything good? Do you believe that justice is the rule of creation? Catholics must believe that. It stands to reason. Justice has to win out."

Laurel shook her head. "It would be nice, but I don't think every last Catholic believes that, not about life here on earth."

"I thought they did. Do you?"

"No, I can't say I do."

"Oh. Well, the point is that the two Staynes would gladly dance on her grave, or fight on it. They do more fighting than dancing, if the truth be told. But they won't, because you and I are here to prevent it. They despise me, I'm proud to say. They gave me the sack the moment they found out my father and grandfather had been stewards and the post was mine by rights. I don't mean to sound proud. I should stop talking. You'll think I'm a madman. Have I made you afraid?"

"No. Would they kill me, too, do you think? If they thought no one would find out about it?"

"In an instant."

"Even though it was the Bishop who sent me?"

John looked down, and then into her eyes. "With all due respect, Laurel Bybank, if you fell in the river today, do you think the Bishop would come down and read the funeral service? Not bloody likely, if you'll forgive my French. I would mourn, and Mistress Alice. No one else."

Laurel tried to smile. "I don't think you should tell me anything more."

"I've told you everything. May I give you some tea? I've a cave under a tree not fifty steps from here. And you needn't rush. The Staynes sleep until after four, and when they wake up they stay in their rooms grumping and sucking down tea and sherry until six or later. Then they go up to Mistress Alice's room and terrify her. My cave is dry as dry, and you're welcome."

Laurel shook her head. "Thank you for your invitation, but I think I shouldn't."

"Quite right, too. Only a foolish, imprudent girl would climb down into a cave with a stranger. Just remember to your comfort that I'm here watching over you. It's a steward's work. You may see me in the hall late one night. I break in on the first of every month and look about. That's how I found you were coming. I read the letter and noted it down in my record book. Care to see it? Your name's in it."

He took two steps to a tall oak and reached his hand into a hole and took out a large book wrapped in oilcloth. He unwrapped it and handed it to her. "Page 43," he said.

She turned to page 43. It was divided into days, starting with December 1. Directly beneath the date was a weather report, "Cloudy, north wind after noon," and a list of comings and goings around the manor. Below that was written, *NIGHT PROWL, DECEMBER,* and under that, "Discovered letter to Bishop Hargreave from Lord and Lady Stayne asking maid for Mistress Alice. Orphan preferred. To be expected."

A piece of envelope was sticking out between the pages at the end of the book, with two lines of a poem showing at the top of it.

THE MAIDEN AT THE WINDOW

My Lady's tower window shines above,
While I, her Steward, watch in ceaseless love.

John took the book out of her hands. "Mr. Lloyd doesn't keep proper records," he said. "This is the only one anywhere. They're turning the household into a complete ruin. You'll see. He doesn't know the first thing about being a steward, not the first. The Staynes are letting everything decay. Plunderell Manor should employ thirty, counting the outdoor staff. How many have they? Five. The girl who stirs the soup makes the beds. Whoever heard of that? Complete ruin and disorder." He put the book back into the tree.

"I should probably go," Laurel said.

"I'm talking too much."

"No, no, not at all."

"I'll see you to the edge of the wood."

"Thank you."

They walked down the road in silence until they could see the river. "There'll be ice enough to cross on in a week," he said. "The bridge was built out of stone from the Saltfield quarry. The dock there to the left of it is fifty years old, 1803. Before the Staynes arrived, we kept it clear underneath. Now see the way the wood floating in the river has jammed itself against the posts? But that's none of your concern."

He reached into his pocket and took out a small wooden horse wrapped in a piece of rabbit fur. "This is for Mr. Regius. He's the stablemaster. You'll give it to him? It's his knife I carved it with. You must tell him I held it just the way he showed me, and never cut myself once. See my hands? He's in the stable, and will be your only friend on the staff. There's Helen, but she's too stupid to trust."

"It's beautiful."

"Do you think so?"

"Oh, yes."

He blushed. "I might want to carve something for Mistress Alice someday, but it would have to be perfect, so I never shall."

"Do you see her when you come prowl?"

He shook his head. "They keep her locked in her room night and day. It would be simple enough for me to climb up the drainpipe, but I would never do that because it would be peering in on her without warning." He put his hand in his pocket. "Have you money? It's a steward's job to make certain his staff is never flat." He held up a penny. "Here. Never fear, it's not my last."

Laurel put her hands behind her back. "No. Thank you. I can't take money I don't earn."

John smiled. "Who taught you that?"

"My second mother. She raised me until I was six."

"You never knew your first?"

"No. She was sick unto death and left me in a basket on the bank of the river Trier, tied to a laurel bush by a ribbon, because she knew Granny Piersall came fishing there every day and would find me. That's how I was named. Now I'm talking too much. Would you mind very much if I asked you a question?"

"Absolutely not."

"It will sound rude, I know."

"No, it won't."

"Do you believe yourself to be a good man?"

John wrinkled his brow and looked up into the trees for a few seconds, and then he looked at her again. "I don't know. Do I seem to be the other way?"

"Oh, no, not at all. It's just that Granny Piersall used to tell me never to trust a man who thought he was good, and I want to trust you."

An owl came gliding along the road, very low to the ground, and swooped up at the last minute and landed in the tree over their heads, sending down a shower of bits of ice.

Laurel laughed and shook herself and ran toward the bridge.

2

HALFWAY UP THE HILL, Laurel stopped and turned around. It was getting colder every minute, and the clouds were beginning to build up for snow. Clumps of ice, like lights, drifted slowly down the river. Hanging on the horizon was a line of black smoke, from a train on the Saltfield track. "God, please grant me strength and courage, and make me smart enough to know what to do."

She looked at the tall oak tree where John Frame had stopped her. Was he sitting at the top of it now, watching her? She started to lift her arm to wave, but then stopped and turned around and looked at the manor house. It made her think of St. Ambrose Chapel, where Father Simpson had said Mass every second Sunday. He called the chapel "St. Squalid's on the Hill," but only when they were alone together. St. Squalid's wasn't nearly as large as Plunderell Manor, but it looked just as dark and miserable and smelly.

"You couldn't make it any uglier," she said softly, and started to walk toward it. "But it's not a factory. I must remember that. And it's not a coal mine, either."

She thought about the factory towns she had been through in the last five days, rotting towns full of thin, pale little children sitting in doorways while their big brothers and sisters, ten and eleven and twelve, stepped over them on their way to the factories or the mines. Always, some of the working children were drunk. Well, she couldn't blame them. Factories were the perfect places for crippling children. Coal mines were more suited to killing them. Father Simpson's last funeral had been for a girl who had fallen into the belts while she was sorting coal. It happened all the time. Sometimes, you didn't even get the body back. It was shipped with the coal to Argentina or Massachusetts.

Plunderell Manor might be an awful place run by awful people, but it wasn't a factory and it wasn't a coal mine. It had stoves and fireplaces and food. She would have her own bed, and regular meals, and work to do. She wouldn't have to feed pieces of tin into a machine, or pick up steel shavings from an oily floor, or slide under looms to make sure the threads were running straight, or stand over a coal sorter, kicking the big lumps into a crusher.

She reached into the inside pocket of her cloak and felt for the letter Bishop Hargreave had written to Lord and Lady Stayne. It was wrapped in oilcloth to keep it dry, and she didn't have to unwrap it to read it, because she knew it by heart.

Most Esteemed Lord and Lady Stayne,

Receive a Bishop's blessing! My heartfelt thanks for your good letter of 14 December, and for your generous contribution to our Cathedral Tower

Fund, a High Goal, if I may venture a lighthearted remark, and dear to the hearts of the pious faithful. Also, good thanks for your inquiry as to my health. I am, praise God, in the rosiest of conditions, except for the occasional case of the sniffles, one price of living in a fallen world. Alas!

Happy Day! I have found just the girl you asked for, an orphan girl of Irish parentage, to judge from her flaming hair and sea-blue eyes, faithful, simple of heart, obedient, to be maid to your niece. Though this creature has not been in my personal employ, I have every confidence that she is as honest and trusting as one is likely to find in these grim days near the End of the Age.

Raised by a pious countrywoman until she was seven or so, the child has since spent her time in the service of a plain country priest, now gone to his Heavenly Reward, without complaint or repining. (I refer, of course, to the girl's attitude, though Father Simpson's pious resignation is also beyond question.)

The girl's name is Laurel Bybank, and she will carry a copy of this letter signed in my own hand so that you will know her for a certainty. I trust that she will give the highest satisfaction, I covet further correspondence with you, and I remain,

Ever, Yours Faithfully,

Francis R. T. Hargreave, Bishop

She came to the top of the hill, where the road divided. To her right was the manor house, and to her left the iron gate into the side yard. The house was dark stone, with three long rows of windows across the front. The shutters were gone, the metalwork under the first-floor windows had been pulled loose, two stone basins by the door had been dug up and set on and against the front wall, the greenhouse, which had been attached to a low porch at the south corner of the house, had been taken apart and the pieces stacked in the flower beds, and the fountain in front of the entrance was now just a hill of stones with some pipes sticking up through it. There were little mounds of dirt all over the front lawn, as if somebody had been burying an army of dogs and cats.

The house seemed dead. No curtains on the windows, no lights, no sounds, nothing moving anywhere.

Laurel walked quickly down the left fork, through the wide gate, and into the yard. It smelled of hay and horses and chickens. A rooster scratched in the dirt next to the wicket leading to the garden. Next to him was a huge pile of dead vines from the summer. A woman came out through the wicket carrying two headless chickens. She walked across the yard and went in through the kitchen door, slamming it behind herself.

Laurel walked to the back of the yard, where the stables were, and in under the low hanging roof. "Mr. Regius?" she said softly.

There was a lantern burning in a stall in the back, and she went to it. A man was there, bent over, holding a horse's hoof between his knees and trimming it with a hooked blade knife.

"Sir?"

He looked up. He had blue eyes and lots of white hair. "Laurel Bybank? It must be. Who otherwise?"

He put the horse's hoof on the ground and straightened up. "Francis Regius. At your beck and call."

"How do you do. I have a message from John Frame."

Mr. Regius held up his hand, pushed the horse farther into the stall, and slid the gate shut. "When did you last eat?"

"This morning. At a farm just this side of Ferwick. The wife was very generous. I don't need food right away."

Mr. Regius took off his leather apron and hung it on a nail. "All the same, we'll see if we can wedge in a bit."

He blew out the lantern and took her hand and led the way out of the dark stable and across the yard and through a low door in the back corner of the house. "Around this way and then to the right," he said, and they entered a room with a table and two benches. "This is where the yard folk ate, in earlier days." He struck a match and lit the candle on the table. "Rest. I'll not be long."

Laurel put her satchel on the table and sat down on the bench and slid to the corner. It was nice to be where it was a little warmer. She leaned her back against the wall, pushed her legs out, closed her eyes, and immediately fell into a quick, clear dream. John was giving her a tour through St. Anne's Church, from the tower to the cellar. He didn't know as much about it as she did, but he was having such a good time trying to explain everything that she just let him do it.

She woke up. Mr. Regius was sliding a bowl of barley soup in front of her. There was a pitcher of hot water on the table, and a pot of tea and a cup. "Drink it down slowly," Mr. Regius said. "There are nice sweet bits of fat in it."

"Are Lord and Lady Stayne still asleep?"

Mr. Regius smiled. "John Frame has given you the drill."

"He told me they slept afternoons."

Mr. Regius took a cup out of his pocket and poured himself some tea. "Their stumps are still in bed."

Laurel ate in silence until all her soup was gone. "Thank you. That was most awfully good. I beg your pardon for falling asleep waiting for you. I can assure you, I never fall asleep when there are duties to be done. I have many vices, I confess, but sloth is not one of them."

Mr. Regius shook his head. "You're too young and too poor for vices."

"Not so. I only wish I were. I'm vain and willful, and I trust too much my own strength."

"More soup?"

"No, thank you. People will sometimes boast of their sins, you know. There was a man in our parish, who has died long since, God rest his soul, who made up ditties about the things he did and sang them in the confessional. Cold sober."

Mr. Regius placed a square, gooey candy in her hand. It was gold-orange in color, and it had bits of lint stuck to it. "I've held this for your coming. It's clean, I promise you."

"Thank you. It's most kind of you to give me such a welcome."

"The Duke of Kent came here when I was a boy. You're the most important visitor since."

Laurel put the candy in her mouth and chewed it. It was apricot, and very sweet.

"I wish I had more," Mr. Regius said.

She reached into the inside pocket of her cloak and took out the little horse wrapped in rabbit skin. "John wants you to know that he carved it with the knife you gave him, and that he held the knife just the way you showed him and never cut himself once."

Mr. Regius smiled. "Did he tell you that, now?"

"Yes, he did."

Mr. Regius took it from her and held it next to the candle and looked at it carefully, turning it over and over in his hands. "Very horsey," he said.

"Yes."

"Bone for bone, wouldn't you say?" He set it carefully on its legs next to the teapot and took his hands away. It didn't fall over. "That's the test," he said.

"John didn't complain to me of the cold," Laurel said. "Or of anything at all, but his lips seemed a bit blue. I kept him standing still a long while."

Mr. Regius picked up the horse again and wrapped it carefully. "I venture it was the other way about, and he kept you. If he needs another coat, he'll ask for it. He has three, but won't wear any of them because he can't climb a tree in one."

Laurel took a sip of tea. "He said this house was a prison."

"True."

"He said they want Mistress Alice dead."

"They might."

"If that's true, why would they send for me?"

Mr. Regius shrugged his shoulders. "Rest assured, there's no use trying to make sense of what they say or do. Nor do you have to. Watch them, is all. Don't be taken in. Be as wise as a serpent and as innocent as a dove."

"St. Matthew's Gospel."

Mr. Regius looked at her. "So?"

"The tenth chapter."

"They let Catholics read the Bible, do they?"

"Why would they not? Protestants have very peculiar notions of Catholics, I think."

"We do." He smiled. "Especially the Irish ones."

"I don't know I'm Irish. Not that I would regret it. The Irish are a good people."

"Whether you are or no doesn't signify. They'll see your red hair and know you are. No matter. Take my advice. Play the simpleton. Look willing and stupid, and never be off your guard."

"Will I be her only servant?"

"First and only for over a year now. She won't know what to do with you at first, being locked up all that while alone."

"Do you ever see her?"

"Not since the day they came, the week her grandfather passed on. They shut her up in a back room, between the upstairs servants' hall and the storage rooms. You'll see the place soon enough."

"What does she do alone?"

"Mends and eats, I suppose. They bring her books, but she gets no letters and sends none. Upon a time I would stand out under her window late and listen for her, and search the ground in the morning for messages thrown down. John's idea. Never a thing, never a sound. They may give her strong drink at night."

Laurel's heart suddenly started beating fast, and she felt the blood in her face. "Shouldn't the magistrate be called?"

"Our magistrate eats here every Tuesday. Eats and

drinks until his man carries him home. And Sundays, after church, they have the Reverend Father Grote-Pinckney at the table. They tell him stories about her and stuff him until his eyes bulge out, and send him home with a box of pastries."

"Dear Jesus," Laurel said, "it makes a person wonder at what people do."

Mr. Regius shook his head. "Don't think of what others do. Think of Laurel Bybank, what she must do to save her mistress."

3

Mr. Regius led Laurel outside into the dark yard. There was a cold wind, and it had started to snow. "I thank you for your kindness," she said. "The soup was more than good. I'll come and visit you when it's daylight, and see your horses."

"Don't make promises. They're certain to curb you. You may not step in this yard again until Easter."

"Oh." She took a deep breath and let it out slowly. "I wish I could leave you with something for remembrance."

He touched her arm. "You are the hope of this house, Laurel Bybank. Someday I'll boast of sitting at table with you your first night here. When the happier times come."

"I'll pray that you can." She looked up at the back wall of the house. "Is her room somewhere there?"

"The high, small window, but it's unlit. Lord Stayne don't let her light her own lamps."

"So she's there in the dark?"

"Until he comes."

A shiver ran up Laurel's back. "I'll do all I can for her. It's a great comfort to me that I'm not alone this side of the river."

"Don't build on me. They have me in Saltfield tonight to fetch back a new horse in the morning. Tomorrow they could drive me off, or I be dead. I'm an old man. I can't see why they keep me."

"John says you're magic with horses. If they drive you off, you could go to his cave. He says it's dry as dry."

"Not this old man. I'll go into the ground only once."

A door opened in the side of the house, and a man's shadow fell on the snow. "Look there," Mr. Regius said. "It happens every night. He stands on the kitchen step drinking his beer and showing the cook his manly figure."

The shadow was long and sharp. Laurel took hold of Mr. Regius's hands and kissed them. "Shall I go around through the back gate and come in through the front?"

"No. Go directly. If he asks, say you came to the stable and I took you and gave you soup. He can't do me any harm, and it's the truth."

Laurel let go of his hands. "God be with you," she said, and walked quickly along the side of the house toward the kitchen. When she got to the door, her heart was pounding. Mr. Lloyd looked down at her without moving. He had on a black formal suit with a black tie and white gloves. "Laurel Blankback," he said, wiping his mouth.

"Yes, sir."

"You went for a swim in the river on your way. Is that what kept you?"

"No, sir. I beg your pardon for being tardy."

"Blankbacks get special privileges? Is that what I am to understand?" He had a soft voice, with a tiny lisp in it.

"No, sir, I don't expect anything out of the ordinary. If it please you, the name is Bybank."

"That's what I said."

"I misheard. I often do stupid things like that."

"Indeed you did mishear. Blankback, Blybank, Bankbank, who's to care as long as you learn where to empty the pot in the morning. Isn't that the gospel?"

"Pardon, sir?"

"Mr. Lloyd is what you call me."

"Yes, Mr. Lloyd."

He drank down the rest of his beer. "I passed you in the woods today. You stared at me, nothing less. Now you pretend you've never seen me."

"I beg your pardon, Mr. Lloyd."

He narrowed his eyes and looked down at her, and she kept her eyes on his soft white gloves. She wasn't afraid of him, not a bit, which surprised her. He made her think of a stunted rooster she had once killed for Sunday dinner.

"You can tell the devil by his lies, missy. Come along inside. And let's not try to heat the whole outdoors."

Laurel shut the door behind her and looked around. There were two others in the kitchen, a cook and her helper. The cook, a big woman about forty, wore a black dress with a white apron and a lace cap. Her helper seemed to be about sixteen or seventeen. She wore a gray dress with a small white apron and a tiny cloth cap. When Laurel caught her eye, she winked.

Mr. Lloyd banged his glass down on the stone sink. "No more cutting and plucking and stirring for the nonce," he said. "Look at this creature I've just brought in out of the snow. I promised you a witch, correct? What Albert Lloyd promises, Albert Lloyd delivers. Devil's child, straight from the arms of an old priest out of a wandering bitch. Says her mumbo-jumbo prayers every day. Redheaded Irish from head to foot."

He pointed his finger at her. "Put your satchel down and turn yourself around so we can see you. Not that way, my sly little thing. I'll not let you put a curse on us, turning to the left. Right. Right. Good. Now give us a greeting."

Laurel curtsied. "I'm very pleased to know you."

"Tell them where you've come from."

"My last place of employ?"

"What else?"

"St. Anne's Rectory in Gravesbury. I was housekeeper to Father John James Simpson."

Mr. Lloyd looked at the cook's helper, making her blush. "He put a tattoo of St. Vitus on her rump, and other saints on other parts, that's certain. One of the Popes invented tattoos, you know, so the Devil's children would know one another. Invisible to the eyes of Christians."

Laurel bit her lip. She despised people who made stupid remarks about the Catholic Church. Father Simpson had taught her never to let her anger show, but she was sure it did, anyway.

Mr. Lloyd clapped his hands. "Back to your tasks now. Shift your bones. I will go up and discover from his Lordship what he wants me to do with this baggage."

He looked at Laurel. "And you, don't let me come back and find Mrs. Winter railing at you for getting under her feet. We keep our own little paradise here, and we won't have anyone coming and spoiling it."

He left, and Laurel stepped into the corner next to the sink, looked down at the floor, and prayed a brief prayer for strength. Then she thought about Alice Plunderell locked in the dark at the back of the house, and felt the first touch of love for her.

She lifted her head and looked around the kitchen. It was very big, with a high wooden table in the middle, so you could stand up straight while cutting or rolling out dough. Two brass lamps hung down from the dark ceiling. Between the lamps was a wooden rail full of hooks, with pots and strainers and grates hanging from them. They all looked a little greasy, and one pot had rust on the handle. The floor around the table was swept, but there were crumbs and peelings and bones in the corners. Even the wall she was leaning against felt gritty and greasy. She wanted to get a bucket of hot water and some brushes and soap and scrub the place down.

Mrs. Winter, who was cutting a lamb joint, looked up. "You, missy, how long do you intend to stand there?"

Laurel took a step away from the wall. "May I help, Mrs. Winter?"

"Likely not, but we'll try you on something simple. Can you tell boiling water when you come on it?"

"I believe so, Mrs. Winter."

"Then see after the kettle."

Laurel went to the stove, reached across to the kettle,

and lifted the lid. "Half full and on the simmer," she said.

"You say?"

"It's near boiling. Shall I fix tea?"

"Shall you what?" Mrs. Winter cracked the joint, cut the shank loose, held it up in the air, and waved it at her. "Fix tea? I know your sort. Wedge in here in your fancy old woman's cloak and expect to be making tea first thing. Is that the way your priests teach you to act?"

Laurel put the lid back on the kettle and put her hands behind her back. "No, Mrs. Winter. I beg your pardon. I didn't mean to push myself ahead."

"Shake some biscuits onto a plate for his Lordship's tray."

Laurel went to the cupboard and opened it up. The shelves were full of sacks and plates and cups and dirty jars. She took out the nearest thing she could find to a biscuit tin, and opened it. There was a dead mouse inside. She closed it again and put it back. "Mrs. Winter? If I may know where I should look?"

Mrs. Winter pressed her thin lips together and smiled. "Back to your corner, missy. Helen? You know a biscuit tin when you see one. Lay his Lordship a plate. The ones I made just yesterday, with the South Seas coconut topping. And pile them high. Don't stint."

Helen dropped the chicken she was plucking, gave a quick curtsy, and ran out of the kitchen. A minute later she came back with a plate full of little cakes with crumbly white frosting.

"Very good, Helen, very trim indeed," Mrs. Winter said.

Helen put the plate down on the corner of the table and went back to her chicken.

"And you such a young girl, too," Mrs. Winter said. "Be schooled by me. Don't take a fancy to this new one. She'll be out in the snow in under a month, you can depend on it. And none of us the loser."

Laurel looked down and waited. Her legs were stiff and tired. She was sorry she had let herself sit down before.

Five or ten minutes passed.

Mr. Lloyd looked in the door. "Helen? His Lordship will have High Tea in his room in ten minutes. Do you know what that means? Ten. One more than nine? One fewer than eleven? Show me your hand."

Helen held up her right hand. There were feathers between her fingers.

"And the other one, dear girl. Good, good. As many minutes as you have fingers on both hands. Can you remember?"

"Yes, Mr. Lloyd."

"Excellent. What a splendid mind you have, after all. Blankback? Follow me."

Laurel grabbed her satchel and followed him down the hall toward the front of the house, through a pair of swinging doors, and into the dining room. A single candle stood on the oak table in the middle of the room. Next to the candle was an empty brass fruit bowl the size of a laundry basket. The drapes had been taken down and stretched on the floor in front of the windows and cut apart.

Mr. Lloyd opened a pair of sliding doors and went out into the entrance hall. "Shut these behind you."

Laurel shut the doors, which were very heavy and hard to move, hitched up the front of her dress, and ran after him up the curving staircase. On the second-floor landing was a plaster statue of ten or fifteen little cupids climbing all over each other. At first she thought they were angels, but then she saw that one of them had his foot in the face of the one under him. He was grinning.

Mr. Lloyd led the way along a wide hall, stopped at a door, knocked, and walked in. Laurel followed him. The room smelled of cinnamon and cigars and coal gas. Oil lamps with red globes hung on the walls.

"The girl," Mr. Lloyd said.

"Thank you, Mr. Lloyd. You may go."

Mr. Lloyd left, closing the door softly, and Laurel and Lord Stayne looked at each other. His mouth was big and his lips were fat and purple. He leaned against one arm of his red leather chair. "Laurel. You're here."

"Yes, my Lord."

"How good."

"Thank you, my Lord."

"Oh, we have been looking forward to your arrival with happy anticipation. Did you bring the snow with you?"

"It snowed a bit in Northbridge yesterday, my Lord, but that was early morning, and it soon changed to rain."

"Did it, now? How interesting. Come closer. Still closer. Put your satchel down next to you. Take off your cloak. Untie your hair. I want to see if Bishop Hargreave was telling the truth about its flaming color. Ha-ha-ha. Merely a witticism, of course. We must always believe our Bishops, mustn't we? Go on, let it down."

Laurel took off her cloak and unpinned her hair.

"Well, that is a good strong rust, isn't it? Have you a match for my cigar?"

"No, my Lord. I'm sorry. Shall I fetch one?"

"No no no no. I have one here. Matches can be very dangerous, did you know that? Young women shouldn't carry them about. I heard a story just the other day of a fourteen-year-old child who burned herself to a crisp. Nothing left of her but some bits of ash, poor thing. You're fourteen, aren't you?"

"I believe so, my Lord."

"You don't know?"

"My Granny Piersall didn't know when she took me in. I was a foundling."

"Dead, I take it? Your granny?"

"Yes, my Lord."

"Can't be helped. We all must die. The great thing is to be prepared for it when it comes. I hope you are."

Remembering to look stupid, Laurel tilted her head to the left and looked at a lion head mounted on the wall beside the bed.

Lord Stayne smiled. "Ever seen one of those before?"

"It's very big, my Lord."

"One shot and he dropped like a stone."

"Very furry, too."

Lord Stayne took a silver matchbox out of his pocket and lit his cigar. Laurel began to feel a little bit sick. "Shall I put more coal on the grate, my Lord?"

"Your priest taught you to keep him warm, did he?"

"He was subject to chills, my Lord, and once he got cold, it took half a day to warm him up again."

"Poor fellow. Yes, stoke it up by all means."

Laurel went to the stove and knelt down and closed

her eyes, hoping the sick feeling would go away. Slowly, it did. She opened her eyes and began laying pieces of coal on the grate one by one.

"Serving in the house of a Lord is a new thing for you," Lord Stayne said. "The higher, more refined matters of life are a closed book to you. Poetry. Art. Setting the table properly. You read and write?"

"Yes, my Lord. Father Simpson's eyes were very weak, but his interest in books never ceased. I read to him, without much understanding, of course."

"Do you correspond with anyone?"

"No, my Lord."

"How sad. Do you know who your father was?"

"No, my Lord."

"How sad. Your mother?"

"Illness caused her to leave me in the care of others when I was very young."

"So now she is in heaven?"

"Yes."

"How dreadful. Well, of course, good for her, but dreadful for you. A girl without her mother to look out for her. I daresay you look forward to that Glorious Day when you will be together with her in that Splendid Celestial City Beyond the Clouds, where the Angels sing around God's Golden Throne?"

Laurel laid the last piece of coal on the fire and stood up slowly. "She's close to me day and night, my Lord. She pleads my case before the saints and angels."

"No doubt. Come here and stand in front of me again. No. Don't pin your hair back up."

She went to him and stood with her arms at her sides. He took the cigar out of his mouth and carefully examined it. Then he leaned back and pushed his feet out. He was wearing shiny black boots. "The way you feel about your mother is just the way a good little Catholic girl should feel. Your new mistress will be pleased with you. I refer not to Alice Plunderell but to Lady Stayne. Do you understand that?"

"I believe so, my Lord."

"Take it to heart. That extra lump on your chest? A goody bag? Spill it out on my lap. I'm not a thief. I shan't keep it."

Laurel did as she was told.

"Well, well," Lord Stayne said. "What is this I see before me? Shillings? Seven of them. Heavens, you're quite wealthy. What is this stone? An arrowhead? You were in America among the Red Indians?"

"No, my Lord."

"And chalks. I used to collect chalks as a child. Wherever did you find the blue one?"

"The Easton caves, my Lord."

"I'll keep it safe for you. And the pink one, too." He put them in his pocket and stuffed everything else back in the pouch and gave it to her. "Now, for the satchel. Don't be shy. Let's see what's in it."

Laurel knelt down and untied it.

He pulled his feet back. "Empty it out. Don't be embarrassed. I have rights in these matters."

Laurel took her things out and laid them on the floor: stockings, underdrawers, a shift, a piece of soap, and a mending box.

"No witch's kit? Bats' eyes? Lizards' tails? Hanged man's toes with the nails still growing? Ha-ha-ha. Just being witty again. Put it back. We have hidden treasure in our house just as you have in your little pouch. I will have occasion to tell you about it in due time. You will have your very important part to play, I promise you. Can you believe that a simple girl such as yourself could take part in an important venture?"

Laurel shrugged her shoulders and tilted her head to the right. "If you tell me so, my Lord."

He stood up and lit his cigar again and puffed hard on it for a minute. "Who is the master of this house? Do you know?"

"You are, my Lord."

He smiled. "Quite. And Lady Stayne mistress. Mustn't leave her out. We two either keep you in service or we put you out onto the road to starve. No reference, no place, no station. You see that choice clearly?"

"Yes, my Lord."

He laid his hand on her neck. It felt damp and warm. "Laurel, I must tell you that I am utterly taken with you. Shall we be on our way to Mistress Alice? I would take you to Lady Stayne, but she needs rest. She spends herself without stint the entire waking day. Follow me. We will go to dear Alice's room. Come."

Laurel put her cloak back on, repacked her satchel, and hung it on her shoulder. On her way to the door, she noticed a painting leaning against the wall in the corner. It showed a tall, slim young woman with dark hair standing on a balcony overlooking a garden. In the background there was a ruined Greek temple and a river and a forest.

She pulled the door shut behind her and followed Lord Stayne. When they got to the top of the staircase, he stopped and looked at her. "You saw the painting?"

Laurel tilted her head. "My Lord?"

"The picture. In the gold frame."

"Oh. Yes, my Lord."

He smiled. "It's an Idealized Portrait. You wouldn't know what an Idealized Portrait is. It's a picture of Alice Plunderell the way the angels in heaven would like her to be. Not to mention God, of course, who is very angry with her for being the way she is. Very angry He is, let me tell you. It's a birthday surprise for her from her loving aunt and uncle. You will not tell her about it."

He started down the stairs. Halfway down, he met Helen coming up with a tray of tea things. He stopped. "Well, what am I seeing here?"

"Tea and cakes, my Lord."

"For me?"

"Yes, my Lord."

He shook his head. "Not so." He picked up one of the cakes and popped it into his mouth and ate it slowly. "Very good, but surely not mine. My tea, the tea I ordered, was to be brought to my room three minutes ago. Therefore, what you have on this tray must be someone else's tea. But whose? Lady Stayne is still resting. Only one conclusion is possible. You are taking it upstairs for yourself. You are planning to walk to the end of the hall, climb the stairs to the servants' hall, sit in your room, and stuff all of this into your own belly. Am I correct?"

Helen shook her head. "Begging your pardon, my Lord, that was none of my intention at all. Mrs. Winter had me doing the chickens for tonight's chicken-and-lamb pie, and the kettle was short a bit of water, and my fingers were all feathers, which kept me."

"So it is her fault that you were going to bloat yourself

with sweets. Is that the case? Very interesting. And she, also, will be interested in learning that she is the guilty party."

"Oh, please don't tell her that, my Lord."

"You want us to enter into a conspiracy together, you and I, against her?"

Helen pulled in her lips between her teeth. She looked about to cry.

Lord Stayne put his hand under her chin and lifted her head. "Never fear, it will be our secret. Now to save you climbing, you will go straight back downstairs and tell Mr. Lloyd that you are an unprofitable servant and that you do not deserve to hold a position in a distinguished household such as this one. Then say to him that he is to be so kind as to boot your backside across the bridge at dawn, because you have failed in your duty of obedience. Do you think you can remember that?"

"Yes, my Lord. I'll try."

"Do. I would write you a reference if I could, but I would have to be severe, so I'd best give you nothing." He put his hand under her chin. "Obedience. What could be more important for a servant? Yes? Agreed? No, Helen, you can believe me, you will fit in much better in some factory somewhere. Or a woolen mill. Are you grateful for my advice in this matter?"

"Yes, my Lord, I am."

"Good. You should be. What did God put us on earth for, if not to help one another?" He grabbed another biscuit. "Come along, Laurel."

Laurel reached out and touched Helen's arm, and hurried after him.

He crossed the entrance hall in a sort of hopping walk and entered the trophy room behind the stairs. It was a long, narrow room, with wild animal heads and axes and spears and knives all over the walls. Lord Stayne picked up an oil lamp from one of the tables and went through the door at the back of the room and down a long ramp to the back hall.

"Almost there. Stay close! Ha-ha-ha."

He turned right and went along the hall to a narrow wooden stairway. "Don't make too much noise and disturbance. Have a care." They climbed to the first landing, where there was a door. Lord Stayne put his lantern down, reached into his pocket, took out a key, and held it in front of Laurel's face. "I'll just unlock the door and pop inside and tell her you're here. Happy surprise? She doesn't know you've come. She knew you were coming, of course, but not when. We tell her everything she has a right to know, a kindness she does not see fit to return, I might say. That will change."

He smiled a quick smile, put the key in the lock, turned it, stepped inside, shut and locked the door again. Laurel could hear his voice, but she couldn't tell what he was saying. She leaned against the wall, closed her eyes, and saw a vision she had seen many times before, of a crowd moving along a road in the countryside. It was her family, going far, far back into the past, farmers and millers and miners and servants, nameless uncles and aunts and cousins and grandparents, going back two hundred years or more. They were her dream relatives, but their faces were so clear she could have gotten paper and pencil and drawn them exactly.

She was in the middle of the front row, holding hands

with a little girl who was skipping along beside her. Someday, long in the future, she would get married and have babies and they would be part of the crowd, but now was too soon to think of that.

She opened her eyes and shook her head. Marrying and having babies was nothing but a dream, which might or might not come true. Now she had to do her work and make herself a place. God put people on earth for work and hard times, Granny Piersall had told her, and she knew it was true. How else was a girl to grow strong, and make herself ready for heaven?

The door opened and Lord Stayne poked his head out. "Come in, my dear."

Laurel stepped inside and waited by the door. Alice Plunderell was sitting on a wooden chair next to her bed. She had blond hair, parted in the middle and pulled back over her ears, and a round face. She was wearing a green dress with a high neck, and there was a white shawl draped over her shoulders. The bottom of her dress made a perfect half circle out in front of the chair, and she had an open book of maps on her lap. Her eyes were blue.

Laurel curtsied. "I am honored to enter your service, mistress, and I hope I will give satisfaction."

Alice smiled. She made Laurel think of a beautiful baby. She didn't look the least bit like the young woman in the portrait.

Lord Stayne looked at Alice and rubbed his hands together. "Tell us, dear niece, what do you think of your uncle and aunt's goodness to you?"

"You are very generous and kind," Alice said. Her voice was soft, and quite low.

He wiggled his hands in the air. "Think of her as an early birthday present. A generous birthday present from the only relations you have in the world. I daresay you're wondering, now, what we have in store for you next. A trip to some faraway place? A meeting with your Intended in some romantic ruin, a monastery perhaps? Just the proper place? Do such ideas strike home with you?"

"Whatever you think best, Uncle."

Lord Stayne tilted his head back and looked at the ceiling. "Are you blushing, dear child?"

"I apologize, Uncle."

"Two kinds of people blush. Do you remember who they are? I've told you many times."

"Children blush, and women who have done shameful things."

"Exactly. Did you forget that?"

"Yes, I did, Uncle."

"Perhaps you have something to blush about?"

"Please, Uncle, I hope not."

"I, too. I'm going to take myself off, now. Make sure you don't permit your servant to stand idle. She does dozens of things, and you can tell her all your secrets without fear."

He smiled with his purple lips and hopped out of the room, leaving the door unlocked. Alice looked down at her book, and Laurel stood by the door, waiting. It was a neat room, cozy and bright. Between Alice's chair and her bed there was a little night table with a bottle of salts and a glass and pitcher on it. Behind her was a long wardrobe that ran almost to the corner. Against the wall facing the back of the house was a coal stove, set on a low hearth, and a Chinese screen with mountain scenes painted on it, and a writing desk. High above the desk was a small window.

To Laurel's right, drawn a little away from the wall, were a low stool and a workbasket full of mending.

Alice turned the page of her book.

"Mistress? Laurel said. "May I serve you in some way?"

Alice shrugged her shoulders and turned another page. "Some young women would have gone quite out of their minds being locked up as I have been," she said. "Not doing so is a sign of strong character, don't you think?"

"I'm certain it is, mistress."

"Do I look to be in good health?"

"Absolutely, mistress. You're a bit pale, but that comes from being closed in, I'm sure."

"I have some good habits, though I love sweets too much."

"Everyone loves sweets, mistress. I was eating a jelly just an hour ago."

"Am I acting like a baby?"

"No, mistress."

"I think I am. I don't know how to act like a lady. I used to, but I've entirely forgotten. Or at least, that's how it seems." She closed her book and looked up. "Laurel, will you be my friend? I'd be yours in an instant if you said yes."

Laurel's heart thumped, and she felt a sudden rush of fear. "Those I've served have always been kind to me, mistress. I've never had a friend. It might be best if we were just mistress and servant."

"Never? You've never had a friend?"

"Not that I recall. And I think if you've never had one, it's like never having a father and mother. You don't feel the need."

"Will you be mine?"

"Mistress, my second mother, Granny Piersall, always made it a great point that it was better if everyone stayed in his own place in the world."

Alice looked down at her book again. "Well, I'm sure that's very sensible."

"Yes, it is."

"Do you care to do some sewing? Hemming or mending?"

"I'd be glad to, mistress."

"Then needlework it will be. I will sit here and look at my maps, and you will find something to sew. See the basket next to the stool there?"

Laurel went to the stool, but didn't sit down. "Mistress? The last thing in the world I want to do is give you distress."

Alice kept looking at her maps. "No no no. I perfectly understand. Does it never happen, do you think? Mistress and servant becoming friends?"

Laurel shrugged her shoulders. "I don't know. If it happens, I expect it's very rare."

Alice looked up a second and smiled. "Well, then, there's no need to say anything else about it, is there?"

Laurel sat down and began to pick through the pile of mending in the workbasket. The room became absolutely silent. A piece of coal popped on the grate. Laurel found a needle and threaded it with white thread and began fixing the hem of a nightdress, making the tiny stitches that Mrs. Smink, the Altar Matron at St. Anne's, had taught her to make.

"Laurel?"

"Yes, mistress?"

"Would you care to see a picture of my Intended? I think you should learn about my prospects, don't you?"

"Yes, mistress, I do."

Alice got up, put her book on the seat of her chair, lifted the cover of her mattress, and reached in under it. "Aunt and Uncle gave me this picture. They think I let it get burned up by accident. Really what I did was cut it out and make it into a paper doll." She sat down on her bed. "Will you sit here next to me?"

"I think your aunt and uncle might not approve."

Alice held the doll out. "Do you want to hold him a minute?"

Laurel came over to the bed and took the paper doll from Alice's hand. It showed a young man wearing a very elegant linen suit and a flowing tie. He looked about twenty or twenty-one, and he was holding a small shovel.

"Have you ever heard of the Pomfret-Watkin Company?" Alice asked.

"No, I can't say I have, mistress."

"It owns twenty-two coal mines. At least, it did. It could own more now. But as desperately rich as the Pomfret-Watkin family is, each Pomfret-Watkin is pious to a remarkable degree. You must think he's handsome."

"Indeed, mistress." She handed the paper doll back.

Alice got off the bed, kissed the doll, and pushed it back under the mattress. "My uncle and aunt have arranged it all. It's a quite old-fashioned way to become engaged, I suppose, but I don't mind at all. His name is Harold, like his grandfather, the first Pomfret-Watkin, and when he's not up in London he lives in the middle of a great park in Hobson with his mother and his horses. His father died when he was fifteen. He has promised to be a good and faithful husband to me, and a stern but loving father to our children. His hands are a bit stumpy, I suppose, but beyond that, he's quite perfect. And it's character that truly matters. Beauty is fleeting."

She sat back in her chair, took her book back on her lap, and held it tight. "Laurel? What if we were friends in secret? We could tell each other shocking things at night after we were supposed to be asleep, and just be servant and mistress in daylight."

Laurel put her feet together and stood as straight as she could. "Mistress, the life of a girl like me, alone in the world with nothing but her work, well, she has to guard it carefully. Being a good servant is the only claim I have to a place in the world. I will serve you, I think I will even die for you, if it comes to that, but I cannot be your friend."

Alice opened her book. "I shouldn't have asked. Will you forgive me?"

Laurel shook her head. "Mistress, there's no need. I love you."

4

A BELL RANG DOWNSTAIRS.

Laurel looked at the door, and then at Alice. "Is that the supper bell, mistress?"

Alice shrugged her shoulders. "I suppose it must be. Everything's new, with you here."

"Shall I go down? I could take some ashes with me, so it won't be a wasted errand."

"Yes, do."

Laurel shoveled ashes into the bucket next to the stove. "I believe it's lamb-and-chicken pie tonight," she said when she was done. She picked up a lamp, went out the door, and hurried down the narrow wooden stairway. Mr. Lloyd was waiting at the bottom.

"You took your time, missy."

"I beg your pardon. The ashes needed sweeping out."

He grinned and leaned his face toward her. "You believe that God takes care of little Catholic girls, don't you? His Lordship told me that not five minutes ago."

She didn't know what to say. God always saved His faithful people in the end, she knew that, but she also knew that the faithful suffered in this world, and sometimes died young and in pain. She looked down at the brick floor.

He moved his face even closer. His breath smelled strongly of beer. "Well, you'll find out different soon enough. Leave the bucket right where you put it. Lord Stayne wants to see you in the trophy room."

"Yes, Mr. Lloyd." Laurel hurried down the hall and into the trophy room. Lord Stayne was sitting in a brown leather chair next to the fireplace. He smiled and pointed to a low wooden bench in front of him. "Sit down, Laurel. I have decided to tell you something. It is something quite shocking, so you will have to get a firm grip on your little heart. And it will require your entire and full attention. Are you ready to listen?"

"I believe so, my Lord."

He smiled. His teeth were very brown. "I am a Good Christian Man. And my dear Lady Stayne is the best of Christian Women. Moreover, I can see that there is much goodness, of a sort, in you. You look forward to receiving your reward in heaven, do you not, a reward more precious than gold and fine jewels?"

"Yes, my Lord."

"Excellent. I can see into your heart, and I know you are speaking the truth. Now, I must tell you about Alice Plunderell. Alice Plunderell is not like you or me. No, not in the least. To be sure, she prances about with her golden hair and her soft voice looking like an innocent angel, but she is the exact opposite of an angel, if you take my meaning. She has bad blood in her veins. Do you know what bad blood is?"

Laurel stared back at him as hard as she could, so

hard her eyes started to water. "No, I don't think so, my Lord."

"That's nothing to be ashamed of. Only listen close now. Do you know why some people are good, and other people are bad? What makes them that way? Blood. Blood. Good people have good blood, and bad people have bad blood. People with bad blood have children with bad blood. Alice Plunderell's father and grandfather had bad blood. It goes far, far back, all the way to Bible days. Alice's wicked grandfather, in his time, gave money to pirates. Can you imagine that? It's the same as giving it to the devil."

"Good heavens," Laurel said.

Lord Stayne raised his eyebrows. "Dreadful, but true. He gave them money to buy guns and rum, and they gave him their best plunder. Gold and jewels. But, as you know, goodness always overcomes evil. And you, dear child, are to be the instrument of that triumph. You are going to help find the treasure. Isn't that a blessing?"

"Yes, my Lord."

"And once we are in possession of it, we are going to give it entirely to a home for orphans in Ireland, except for one gold ring, which we will put on your sweet little finger, as a remembrance. Isn't that splendid?"

"Yes, my Lord."

"Lucky girl! Now listen carefully. Here's the drill. Alice's evil grandfather made up a little riddle about where he had hidden the treasure chest. Solve it, and you find the chest. According to the riddle, it's where August's mother bids her son goodbye. Odd? Alice told us the riddle, but she's keeping the answer a secret just to torture us and make us suffer. She plans, as soon as she's eighteen, to dig it up and spend every penny of it on sin. She must be prevented, for the sake of her soul. Better to die innocent than to live a life of sin and spend eternity in hell because you wouldn't share the world's goods with your nearest relations."

He stood up, and Laurel did the same. He ran his fingers over her head as if he were stroking a cat. "Run along now, and remember the orphans in Ireland."

Laurel curtsied and got her bucket from the back hall and carried it out to the ash bin next to the stable. It was snowing hard, and there were already two or three inches on the ground. After she had emptied the bucket, she started to walk into the stable to visit Mr. Regius, but then she saw wagon tracks, already starting to fill up with new snow, leading across the yard and out through the gate.

She looked up at Alice's window, a square of light high up in the falling snow. "God save us," she said, and crossed the yard and went into the kitchen. Mr. Lloyd was there, drinking beer, and Mrs. Winter.

"Wondering where little Helen went?" Mr. Lloyd asked.

"No, Mr. Lloyd. I'm here to fetch Mistress Alice's supper."

He pushed the tray along the top of the table toward her. There was a white dish in the middle with a piece of lamb shank and a wet pile of green stuff on it, and next to it a cracked little bowl of yellow pudding with red goo on top.

When she reached out for the tray, Mr. Lloyd grabbed her wrist. "I know what you think, missy," he said. "You think I couldn't see Alice Plunderell ten times a day if I wanted to. I wouldn't waste my time. She doesn't signify in this house. Don't look down. Look at me."

Laurel looked at him. His eyes were glassy and bloodshot.

"She knows it, that she doesn't signify. She would be more than glad to have my services, if she could get them. She calls out my name late, late at night, when nobody else is listening. She thinks I'd be quite the catch for someone with her prospects. But I wouldn't have her. Do you understand that? I wouldn't have her."

Laurel kept looking at him, saying nothing. She thought he might hit her with his free hand, but he let her go. She put her lamp on the tray and picked it up and went upstairs and laid out dinner on the writing table near the stove. Alice waited next to her bed with her hands behind her back. "Shall I show you something?"

"Yes, mistress, by all means."

Alice came over to where Laurel was, and held out a glass globe with a glass daffodil inside. "Here. You may hold it." It looked like a perfect flower in full bloom under clear, clear water. "Put it up to the light. It always brings back summer, even on nights in winter."

"It's beautiful," Laurel said.

"I think so, too. I look at it every day. It's like having my own private garden. My father bought it in Cambridge, America, near Boston. There's a man there who makes them."

Laurel handed it back. "Thank you."

"You're welcome. There's something else." She went to her wardrobe and opened the door and took out a boot. "This is my secret hiding place. Look." She held up a little cage, five or six inches long and three inches high, made out of little sticks. "The Chinese make them," she said. "Of course, theirs are true works of art. This is all patching. Matchsticks and egg-and-bread glue. The Chinese keep pet crickets. Did you know that? That's where I got the idea."

"I didn't know that, mistress. Should you wait to show me that until after dinner?"

"No, no. I had a cricket. He came to me all by himself. I think he jumped from a tree one day, and a sudden wind picked him up in the air and flung him in here. I named him Stormy. I already had the cage waiting, as if some angel had told me he was coming. One night my aunt came in when I had him on my night table, but he was sleeping quietly and she didn't notice, though she stood less than a step away from him as I said my prayers. I believe God kept her from seeing him. Do you?"

"God does more miracles than anyone can count, mistress."

"I believe that, too. I kept him for ever so long. From late fall through the winter and into spring. And all the while he was bright and lively and ate whatever I fed him, in very little bits, of course. And then, from one day to the next, he died. My dear aunt would say it was a pagan thing of me to do, but I had a funeral for him. I made a coffin out of my button box, and decorated it with ribbons, and lined it with a silk panel out of my best petticoat for him to lie on, and painted flowers inside the lid. I was sure that Uncle Percy would leave the door unlocked one night by mistake, and I would be able to go down to the garden to bury him, and three days later he did, which was another miracle. I waited until the very middle of the night, when the train blows its whistle going through Saltfield, and went up to the cemetery garden behind the manor and had a ceremony and even raised a little stone monument. Would you have done something like that, do you think?"

"I don't think I would have been brave enough, mistress. I'm bound I would have wanted to."

"Do you think I was brave?"

"Yes, I do."

Alice put the cage back in the boot and shut the closet door. "I should eat now. They get very upset when I don't eat everything they provide, and they can always tell."

5

LAUREL HAD JUST BEGUN BRUSHING Alice's hair when Lady Stayne came into the room. She was a short woman, with wide shoulders and dark eyebrows. She wore a black satin dress with little loops at the ends of the sleeves that hooked around her thumbs and cut into the fat on the backs of her hands.

Laurel put the brush down on the dresser and curtsied.

"So," Lady Stayne said. "You have arrived."

"Yes, thank you, Lady Stayne."

"You know your tasks?"

"I believe so, my Lady."

Lady Stayne smiled. "Life is brief, and we ought not spend time on vanities. Moral improvements are the only ones that matter." She looked around the room. Her eyes were very small, black, and buried deeply in her head. She smiled. "Niece? You are well?"

"Yes, I believe so, Auntie."

"No reason under heaven why not. We take the best of care of you. Lots of good soups, lots of bowel food, and we keep you out of harm's way, as anyone will testify. Still, and in spite of all our best efforts, Death could pay a visit at any time. I have spoken of that often, and told you that you must be ready at all times. So I have discharged my duty in that line. Would you agree?"

"Yes, Auntie."

"The first hour of a creature's frail life, as I have often said, is none too early to begin preparations for eternity. Satan lies in wait for the wicked and the weak, and the fires of hell burn night and day. True?"

"Yes, Auntie."

She looked at Laurel. "And you? We must concern ourselves with your soul, too. Catholics go to hell. From the Pope down. Just because you are simple and ignorant and weak, God will not forgive you for being a child of Rome. You may do as you wish, of course, but my advice is that you join the Anglican Church immediately. It's on your head, not mine."

Laurel looked down at the floor and said nothing.

Lady Stayne clapped her hands. "Alice will now approach the Throne of God."

Alice went over to the bed and knelt down next to it, folded her hands, and bowed her head.

"Eyes closed?"

"Yes, Auntie."

"Heart contrite?"

"Yes, Auntie."

"Intentions pure?"

"Yes, Auntie."

"Nothing held back?"

"Nothing, Auntie."

"Then steer your heart toward the Holy Harbor of Prayer. Oh, thou Majestic and Exalted God, whose judgment is swift and terrible upon the sinner and the disobedient one, save by Thine Infinite Grace thy child Alice. Forgive her for keeping secrets from those who love her best, and cause her to change her ways before it is too late. Amen, amen, and amen. Now, into bed."

Alice climbed into bed and pulled her blankets up to her chin.

"I have a nice bedtime story for you," Lady Stayne said. "I am going to tell you a little tale for the instruction and uplift of your soul, a sweet little animal story, with a lesson for those as are ready to listen.

"Once upon a time there was a little cow, and her name was Alice. She was rather pretty, for a cow, but vain, very vain. One day her grandfather, the old bull who lived in the next field, called her to him and told her about a very special place he knew, full of green grass and sweet water. She asked him where it was, and he told her, and then he died. She immediately grew vain and deceitful and greedy, and decided that she would keep it a secret, and when she came of age she would go to that field and eat up the grass and drink up the water all by herself. Now, wasn't that a wicked thing for her to have decided? Wicked and selfish?"

"Yes, it was, Auntie."

"But there's more to the story. Little Alice the cow had a very excellent Auntie Cow, as well as a very fine Uncle Bull, who came to take care of her and keep her safe in the pasture while she was growing up. It cost them much suffering and inconvenience to do this duty, but they never stinted. But do you suppose little Alice

Cow cared a fig about that? Not a bit. 'No matter how nice my dear relations are to me, or how they must sacrifice their comfort to give me care, I will never tell them where the green grass is,' she vowed to herself. Wasn't that a low attitude to take?"

"Yes, it was, Auntie."

"But, out of the kindness of their hearts, her aunt and uncle persisted, returning kindness for abuse, and purchased for her a little red-haired Irish setter dog to keep her company and be her companion, because they knew that the sin in her heart had put her soul in deep, deep danger. Sad to say, there was little left of her soul but worms and festering poisons, due to her sin of selfishness. But all of a sudden she had someone to whom she could unburden her heart. And so that very night she told her little dog where the green grass was, and her heart felt a thousand times lighter, because the acid of sin was no longer burning there, and she could be a happy little cow again. Isn't that grand?"

"Yes, Auntie."

"Quite right. Now, don't let the seed of that story fall on fallow ground, dear child. Take its holy lesson to heart." She put out her hand. "You may kiss me now, and Laurel will put out the lights, all but one. Good." She looked at Laurel. "Come along. Lord Stayne will have a word with you."

Laurel followed her through the door. Lord Stayne was waiting on the landing in a heavy wool coat, with a candle at his feet. He smiled and rubbed his hands together. "Well, Laurel," he whispered, "tonight you will earn a star in heaven. When you go back in the room, you will find out from Alice where the treasure is, and then you will come and tell me. It must be done before midnight. It's snowing, which is fine weather for confessions. And for other surprises, I might just as well tell you, ha-ha-ha. I will put a candle at the bottom of the stairs to assist you in finding my room. She must say exactly where August's mother bids her son goodbye, and she must say it twice, so you can't forget. Then you come to me and repeat her words."

"If she tells me, my Lord."

Lord Stayne grabbed her arm and pushed his thumb hard into it. "She will tell you. You will make her, or be thrown out into the snow."

He let go and picked up the candle and led Lady Stayne down the stairs. Laurel went back into the room and shut the door quietly.

Alice sat up in bed. "What did he say?"

"He wants me to get you to tell me where the treasure is."

"Oh. Well then, I must, mustn't I?"

Laurel shook her head. "No, it's not wrong to keep a secret."

"If I don't, they'll take you away. Will you come sit on my bed? I'm certain they won't come back."

Laurel went and sat down where Alice had made room.

"Sometimes I think they're cruel on purpose. Did they tell you anything about my grandfather?"

"They said he gave money to pirates."

Alice started to play with the ribbon on her nightgown. "Well, in a way it's true. He knew all manner of sea captains. There was one particular friend who had lost his wife and child and wanted to enter some desperate enterprise. That was 1812, when we were fighting with the Americans. What he did was more like going to war than piracy, Grandfather said. When it was over, his friend brought him back a chest of jewels and coins, and Grandfather hid it. Did they tell you the riddle about where they put it?"

"Where August's mother bids her son goodbye."

"Somebody probably solved the riddle long ago and took it away. Can you guess the answer?"

"No, I don't believe I can, mistress."

"If I tell you, will you believe it and tell my aunt and uncle? Because I don't care if they find it or not, as long as they don't take you away."

"I may not be worth the keeping," Laurel said.

Alice let go of her ribbons and grabbed Laurel's hand. "Yes, you are. Besides, my Intended has jewels to spare. He doesn't need a dowry from me."

"It's true, mistress. He does seem rich enough from what you say."

"I know my aunt and uncle haven't found it, because every time they get a new idea I hear them banging away at one part of the manor house or another. It's comical, really, in a way. So now I will tell you. There is a treasure chest in the cemetery under a square black stone. You must believe me, or else they won't believe you. They're very clever and can see things. And then, as soon as you've told, you must hurry back. I won't be able to blink my eyes until I see you again."

Laurel got up without a word, went quickly to Lord Stayne's room, and knocked on the door. She heard his voice calling out something, and stepped inside. Lady Stayne was sitting with him at a little table. They were playing cards and eating chocolates. The room was extremely hot. Neither of them looked at her.

"She unburdened herself?" Lady Stayne said.

"Yes, my Lady."

"So?"

"There is a treasure buried in the cemetery, under a square black stone."

"Is that all she said?"

"Yes, my Lady."

Lord Stayne looked at her. "In the garden?"

"The cemetery, my Lord."

He smiled. "Just testing. It's what I suspected. It was never in the house." He waved his hand. "We're done with you."

Laurel went back to Alice's room and told her what had happened.

"Did they seem happy with the news?" Alice asked.

"I believe so," Laurel said. "Lord Stayne more than Lady Stayne."

"Good. Thank you. Do you want to go to sleep now?"

Laurel pulled the mattress out from under Alice's bed, got a blanket and coverlet from the closet, undressed as far as her shift, added a bit of coal to the fire, and lay down.

"Laurel?"

"Yes, mistress."

"Would you like to play a game? A guessing game?"

"If you would, mistress."

"What isn't in this room that should be?"

"I don't know, mistress."

"Guess."

"I can't think. I've never been in such a room as this."

"A mirror. There should be an oval mirror on the dressing table. Aunt Salvia told me she had it taken away to keep me from becoming still more vain than I am. I don't think that was kind. The Pomfret-Watkins have a thousand mirrors in their house, I'm sure. Am I pretty?"

"Yes, very."

"How pretty? Like what? They say 'Pretty as a bird,' or 'Beautiful as a rose,' or 'Handsome as a peacock.' What would you say, if you had to?"

"I'd say you were as pretty as a bird."

"What kind of bird?"

Laurel thought for a minute. "A goldfinch."

"Truly? I can hardly wait to see for myself. I think you're quite pretty, too, in case you'd like to know."

Laurel rolled over on her side. "Thank you, mistress."

6

LAUREL OPENED HER EYES. Lord Stayne was stomping around the room swinging a lantern. He came over and poked her in the ribs with his foot. "Get up, Miss Slugabed. Ha-ha-ha. Alice, dear niece? No time to lose. You, too."

"Uncle Percy?"

"The same. Up, up, little sparrow. Time to meet your bridegroom. Did I say bridegroom? Did you hear correctly? You did. Here, I'll light you a lamp, but you must be quiet. No need to wake anyone. Walk about like a lady. You'll be with your dear Harold soon."

Laurel sat up, pulled her blanket around herself, jumped for the Chinese screen, and put on her dress as fast as she could. Then she went over to the stove and pulled on her shoes. Lord Stayne pointed his finger at her. "Something light and airy for your mistress. No delays. Two minutes."

He went out the door and closed it quietly. Alice slid her feet to the floor, keeping the blanket over her knees. "Is it true?"

"I don't know, mistress."

"I mean, it's not a dream."

Laurel shook her head. "Oh, no. Not with both of us in it. I'll find you something warm."

"No. My uncle said it should be something light. I know." She went to the closet and took out a pale blue dress with lacy sleeves and held it up in front of herself. "It may be a bit tight. My bosom has become ever so much larger since early summer."

Laurel shook her head. "Not that one, mistress. There's a snowstorm."

Alice put her hand in the sleeve and looked at her fingers through it. "Perhaps something a little bit heavier."

Laurel went to the wardrobe. "Your Intended's mother will want you in something modest and warm."

Alice put her hand over her mouth. "It's true. I've never met her. I must look sensible."

"We'll take this wool dress, and cover it over with a cloak," Laurel said. "He'll not know. He wants to be away quickly."

Alice shut her eyes. "Whatever you tell me, I'll do."

Laurel held the dress in the air. "Lift up your arms. Good. Sense is more important than beauty. You mustn't come to your Intended sneezing and coughing. Can you button it yourself, and I'll find a cloak?"

Alice started buttoning. "Prudence is everything in a wife," she said. "I should know that."

Laurel found a cloak with a woolen lining and pushed it over Alice's head before she was finished buttoning. Then she took the blanket off her mattress, went to the door, leaned back against it, hitched up her skirt, and wrapped the blanket around herself, poking it up under her waistband so it would stay. After she had tugged at it to make sure it was tight, she went around the room and put out all the lamps but one.

Lord Stayne came into the room and pulled off Alice's cloak. "You make her look like an old woman. Get her a shawl. Come along. No more delays." He threw the cloak onto the bed and went out of the room, and Alice ran behind him. Laurel grabbed her own cloak and put it on, took the heaviest shawl she could find from the wardrobe shelf, said a quick prayer, picked up her satchel, and ran after them.

When she got to the top of the stairs, Lord Stayne was already hurrying down back hall in his hopping walk, with Alice two or three steps behind him. He got to the back corner door and pushed out into the dark. Alice waited for Laurel.

"Thank you, mistress. Wrap this shawl around yourself."

They went out into the yard. There was a strong, very cold wind with bits of ice that cut like needles. "I have a blanket for the carriage," Laurel said. "Don't tell."

They followed the lantern out through the gate and down the hill. Near the bottom, they came upon a carriage with the canvas cover over the driver's box flapping in the wind. Lord Stayne hung his lantern between the horses and climbed up onto the box. The carriage door opened, and Lady Stayne got out. She was wearing a long fur cloak with a white fur collar.

Lord Stayne looked down at her. "This is heavier than I reckoned on."

"No, it isn't."

"I can't see."

"Yes, you can. You know the way. You won't get lost. The whole world trusts you. This is the perfect night. Alice, tell your uncle you know he will take you to a safe place."

"Oh, yes, Uncle."

"See?" Lady Stayne pointed her finger at Laurel. "Hurry. Help your mistress into the carriage. I'm turning to ice here, little anyone cares. You will ride backward, and your mistress forward."

Laurel helped Alice climb inside and then got in herself, and Lady Stayne slammed the door behind them. The window was open, and there was snow on both seats. Lady Stayne reached inside, still wearing her glove. "Kiss your aunt goodbye. We'll pray for you."

Alice leaned forward to kiss her hand, but then a whip cracked and the carriage heaved ahead, throwing Laurel down hard on the floor between the seats. "I'm fine," she said. "Nothing wrong." She got up. The carriage tilted. It seemed to be sliding sideways, but then it straightened up.

"Sit by me," Alice said.

"There's less wind riding backward," Laurel said, lifting herself up and pulling the blanket out from under her skirt. "It might be better if you rode on this bench."

Alice came over next to her, and she tucked the blanket around her. "If the carriage stops," Laurel said, "you must give it back to me right away." She reached out to pull the curtain down, to keep some of the wind and snow from coming in, but it had been removed.

"Have you ever been to London?" Alice asked.

"No, mistress, I haven't."

"Would a person travel to London in this sort of vehicle?"

"I don't believe so, mistress."

"Then my Harold must be at home with his mother in Hobson, and that's where we're going. She has been a widow since Harold's father died."

"Is your blanket tucked in properly?" Laurel asked.

"Yes. Did you ever travel with your priest at night in the winter?"

"Sometimes. It's easier to drive than to ride. You know where you are, if you know the roads well, and you have something to do."

"Have you ever seen anyone die?"

"Yes. It's not frightful. I thought it would be, but it isn't."

"Have you ever seen a baby born?"

"Once, by accident."

"That means you know almost everything in life. What we are doing now is very unusual, wouldn't you say?"

"Yes, it is, mistress. But the angels are watching over us. They can see day or night, snow or rain."

"Like Uncle Percy."

"Even better."

"Would he take my blanket away if he found it, now that he knows how very cold it is?"

"I don't know, mistress, but we'll hide it, anyway."

"I'm going to pull it over my head now to keep my head warm."

"Maybe you can sleep. Let me help."

After a minute, Laurel pulled her own cloak over her

face and began thinking about John Frame. Had he watched as they were driving away? Of course not. It was an infant question. He was in his cave, where he belonged. Tomorrow, when he woke up, the wind and the fresh snow would have covered up the tracks of the horses and the wheels. He was sleeping now, deep underground, where it was warm and cozy.

She fell into a fitful sleep. Once she woke up to find the carriage going very slowly. She reached out to snatch Alice's blanket away, but then the carriage speeded up again. A second time, she felt the carriage slowly turning right. It leaned way over to the left, which made Alice twitch in her sleep, and climbed over some rocks and went on. Laurel fell asleep again and had a vivid dream, full of reds and greens, that she was in Bishop Hargreave's home trying to find him, going from empty rooms to rooms full of animals to hallways crowded with people who wouldn't stop for her.

She woke up. The carriage was stopped. Alice was leaning forward in her seat. Laurel pulled the blanket away from her and sat on it. The door opened. "Come, come. Time to rest. We'll just get ourselves in out of the cold. You won't need your shawl." Lord Stayne leaned his face against Laurel. She could smell the brandy on his breath. "You won't need your cloak, missy. Take it off and follow us."

He pulled Alice behind him and around the carriage. Laurel jumped to the ground, reached back into the carriage and got the blanket and pushed it up between her legs, grabbed her satchel, and hobbled after them. She was wide awake. She knew for certain now that he planned to murder them by freezing them to death. She felt for the money pouch around her neck.

They went through a half-opened door into an old, abandoned monastery. There was a long streak of snow blown across the stone floor. To the left was an arch which opened into a chapel. They crossed a wide hall and entered a long corridor with rooms on both sides. Laurel stepped in front of the fourth one and pulled off her cloak and threw it inside, along with her satchel. Better to be rid of them now, and know where they were, than to let him take them away.

He stopped at a door with a new bolt on it, and pushed it open. "Nothing for my dear niece that is not the best of the best. Come in, both of you. Isn't this fine? Ah, the simple, orderly life of the monk. I have always believed that the poor have an advantage over the rest of us, having nothing to give up. What do you say to that, Laurel? Aren't the treasures of this world a great burden?"

Laurel looked at his shadow against the wall. "Pardon, sir?"

He turned and smiled. "Time for a rest. A nice monk's bed with an excellent rope mattress? Been here forever. Perfect condition. Look around. You have everything a soul needs. A prayer bench. Bookshelves? How lucky. And you'll be out of harm's way. One cannot put too high a price on that."

He went to the hearth and slapped his hand down on it. "Perfect. Nothing less." He turned and left the room and slammed the door and slid the bolt. They heard him cough and walk quickly down the hall. After that, they heard nothing at all.

They were alone together in the black.

"I hope he isn't catching cold," Alice said. "Don't you?"

"Oh, yes."

"How long will it be, do you think, until morning?"
"Not very long."
"Will he come back right at dawn, do you think?"
"Who can say, mistress?"
"What do you suppose?"
"He has his plans, I'm sure, mistress. We must see after ourselves now. I'm standing here by the bed. You must walk toward me and roll yourself in this blanket." Laurel pushed the bed against the wall so that it made a bang. "Can you find your way here, do you suppose? You mustn't permit yourself to get a chill."
"I'm coming. In the spring, when the birds are nesting everywhere, this must be a wonderful scene, don't you think? Very picturesque? Am I getting closer?"
"I'm right here. Reach out and touch me. Good. Now, I will give you this blanket. You have it. I must find something to make a fire. That will give us light, too."
"Do you think you should? My uncle becomes very annoyed when he thinks someone has disobeyed him. What's that clicking?"
"Granny Piersall hated matches," Laurel said. "I have flint and steel. Your uncle saw them when he took my chalks, but he didn't remember what they were. Are you wrapped up properly? If you get too cold, you'll not get warm again."
"Must I sleep?"
"No, mistress. Just try to keep warm."
Laurel got down on her hands and knees and began to feel around for leaves, bits of rope, twigs, or anything else dry that might have been blown in or left behind by mice. She moved her hands very slowly, so that whatever she hit she wouldn't knock away. She touched

something and picked it up. It was a dead beetle, and when its sharp little feet dug into her thumb, she jumped back, flipping it across the room.

"What was that?"

"A scrap of something," Laurel said. "It was wrong of me to throw it away. It would have burned perfectly well."

She moved to the right and ran her hand along the floor next to the wall and began to pick up all kinds of good things, twigs and feathers and leaves and bits of lint, putting them all in her left fist.

"He might be going ahead to meet my Intended and bring him here," Alice said. "He has always had my best interests at heart. He can be severe with me. My Aunt as well. But they want only the best for me. They tell me that almost every day, because they know I forget. He was very brave to take us here in a snowstorm."

"Your aunt wanted it."

"Yes. He hates not to please her."

Laurel came upon a small pile of snow in the corner. She drew her hand back and wiped it on her skirt. She was beginning to shake with the cold.

"What are you doing now?"

"I'm about done collecting. Did you ever see a cottager sparrow?"

"A bird?"

"Yes." Laurel stood up and felt her way to the hearth. "They're ever so tiny, and they build nests on the ground, in the tall grass. The nests are round, like the African huts you see in the missionary papers. Thicker at the top, with a little hole in the bottom for them to climb in and out. It could go on raining for days and days, and the ground turn to muck, but inside the nest it's as dry as a bone. I'm making a little tinder nest. Granny Piersall would collect them and line them up over the door. They were always ready to start a fire on, once you peeled the outside layer. I'm going to make some sparks now. You mustn't be afraid."

"Laurel?"

"Yes, mistress?"

"I don't mean to be timid, but perhaps you shouldn't."

Laurel turned in the direction of Alice's voice. "Mistress? May I tell you? This building could as well be an ice cave."

Alice said nothing more, and after a few moments Laurel turned back to the hearth, laid the steel flat in the palm of her hand, and struck it with the flint. The flash of light showed her where the nest was, and she moved her hand and struck again. Now she saw just where to place the steel, and she hit it a third time. A narrow fountain of sparks went into the thumbhole in her tinder, and after a few seconds she saw a small orange light glowing inside. She put her cheek down on the cold stone and blew gently. The orange light spread, got very bright, started to fade, and then got bright again. A flame as thin and sharp as a needle reached up through the nest, a cone of smoke spinning around it, and then the whole center of the nest was on fire.

The light showed her some twigs and sticks in the corner, and she put them on the fire. Then she saw a branch that had grown through the window and broken off, and slats from a shutter, and part of a shelf. She laid them on, and then glanced at Alice. "You needn't fear," she said. "At worst, a little smoke."

"I'm not afraid," Alice said. "Why should I be?"

Laurel began going around the room breaking up all the furniture that could be broken, a stool with long legs, a small table with a shelf on the bottom, the kneeler piece from a prayer bench, and a line of pegs on the wall that she broke off by hitting them with the kneeler.

"Your uncle left us a goodish bit," she said.

Alice sat and watched, biting the middle finger on her right hand.

"It's good to have light," Laurel said.

"Aren't you cold, with nothing but your dress on?"

"Not too. I'll sit on the hearth."

"You are very very clever."

Laurel looked back at her and smiled. "I'll do everything I can to see you prosper," she said. "Try to sleep."

7

LAUREL SAT ON THE HIGH HEARTH, as close to the fire as she could get. She was very cold. She thought of adding wood, but she was afraid to burn too much too fast. Twice before in her life, she had sat up waiting for morning. Once was the night Father Simpson had died. The other was the night he had baptized twins born too soon. The babies had struggled all night and died together the next morning. That was two winters ago. Or was it three? She couldn't remember. It was hard to think.

She leaned forward, pulling away from the cold wall, and shifted around so that the bottoms of her feet faced the fire. She looked around. There was an alcove high in the wall over Alice's bed. A statue of the Virgin Mother had stood there once, she was sure. A wooden fan stood behind it. Her stomach hurt. She closed her eyes and leaned her shoulder against the wall. She thought of Granny Piersall in the sunshine of heaven. She began to think about her own death. Might she be dead already? She opened her eyes.

If angels went around nights picking up people's souls, they might save the younger ones for last, to keep the old ones from having to wait too long. Some people, maybe most people, might be ignorant that they were dead until the angel came through the door. How would they know? Freezing to death was probably quite easy. She slowly reached out her left hand between the fire and the wall, to see if it cast a shadow. It did.

She shut her eyes and could see her mother quite clearly, leaning over a balcony rail in heaven, looking down. She had her head tilted to the side, like a mother looking down at her sleeping baby. "I must try to get some rest," Laurel said to herself, reaching across to the other side of the hearth and putting a table leg to the fire. "The night must be almost over by now."

When she opened her eyes, there was a dim gray light in the room. The fire was almost out. A smoking bit of wood and a few twinkling coals were all that were left. Her heart jumped. She got off the hearth and added wood and blew on the fire until it was going smartly again.

It was day. Time to start to think. The first thing was to find a way out. She went to the door, took hold of the handle, and pushed. It didn't move. She turned around and leaned against it and pushed again, very hard. Still nothing. She stood there trying to think of her next move, and her eye fell on the little drift of snow in the corner. Where did it come from? She looked directly above it.

There was a small hole in the ceiling. She went over to the corner and looked up. The hole was smaller than her hand. She could see plaster and rocks and maybe a little edge of roof tile, and a piece of blue sky. She went to the fire and pulled out a table leg and brought it back to the corner and rubbed it in the snow. It smoked and steamed and hissed, but she kept rubbing it on the stone floor until it was down to solid wood and quite sharp. She went and stood by Alice's bed.

"Mistress?"

Alice shut her eyes tighter. "Has everything come right?"

"Not yet, but it's day, and I believe I can get us out."

"Truly?"

"Yes."

Alice opened her eyes.

Laurel smiled. "We're alive, and I know how to escape. Through the ceiling. Once I'm outside, we'll have plenty of firewood, and water to drink. Are you thirsty?"

"I usually have tea."

"The monks might have left a whole wall of tea behind."

Alice sat up. "Do you think so?"

Laurel shrugged her shoulders. "Well, it doesn't seem likely, but there must be a kitchen. It's stopped snowing. You can see blue sky through the hole. I want to tip your bed up and climb up it to make the hole bigger."

Alice blinked her eyes slowly a few times, as if she was thinking of going back to sleep. "We won't die, will we? Do you think?"

"Not if we stir ourselves."

Alice rested her head on her knees. "I've been thinking how much a young woman needs a gentleman to see her through this world. Without a good man, the difficulties of this life are beyond the human imagination. You have no Intended."

"No."

"How do you carry on? The image of my Intended hangs ever before me. I brought him with me in the bosom of my dress. Did you see me reach under my mattress first thing?"

"No, mistress. You must have been very quick."

"I was."

"Mistress? We can't take up our journey to him until we get out."

Alice got up, and the two of them swung the bed around and stood it on end in the corner. "Do you think my uncle knew it was a lie, and this is the way he's punishing us?"

"What, mistress?"

"That my grandfather's treasure chest was in the cemetery. Truth to tell, I have no idea in the world where it is. It's my cricket's coffin that's under the stone."

Laurel gave Alice the table leg and climbed the rope mattress with her back to it until her head was just below the ceiling. Then she reached down and Alice handed her the leg again. "Have a care, mistress. Bits of ceiling are going to drop."

She leaned back against the ropes and started banging and poking and scraping. It was hard work, but bit by bit the hole got larger. Once, a large round stone fell without her touching it and bounced around the room like a ball, and when she started working in the hole it had left, a bucketful of plaster and rotten wood dropped on the floor at once. "That black wiry stuff is horsehair," she said. "I've seen masons mixing, so I know."

After a long while, after the hole was big enough for her shoulders, she stepped up higher, which made it easier on her arms.

"Is it big enough yet?" Alice asked. "You wouldn't want to get stuck. Do you think you're being careful enough?"

"Oh, yes, mistress."

"If you fell, what would we do?"

"We'd have to hire a workman to finish the job." She stopped and smiled down at Alice. "I have the shillings, but I'm not sure where I would find him. What do you think? Are we making great progress?"

Alice was squinting. She had a worried expression on her face, but she smiled back. "Yes. Your hair is full of plaster."

"Can't be helped. At least I'm warm."

Laurel worked on for a while, and then decided that the hole was big enough to get through. She climbed higher on the bed and pushed herself out onto the roof. It was cold and clear and the snow smelled clean. There was a tree leaning against the roof, and she worked her way to it and pulled herself up by one of the branches. "I'm safe," she yelled, brushing the snow off her front.

Alice answered, her voice sounding as if it were coming from deep in a cave. "What is there?"

"It's a true cloister. This building goes around a garden, and there's another building, and a hall connecting them. Part of the hospital roof is fallen in. That must be what it is. Ruin everywhere. The garden's just a jungle. Lots and lots of wood."

"Can you see how we came?"

Laurel looked over the low peaked roof toward the forest. "There isn't a track or a mark anywhere. There are fields around, and woods. I'm going to climb down into the garden now and explore a little. I'll try to bring you a happy surprise."

"Just hurry," Alice said, and Laurel climbed down through the tree.

The garden was a wreck. Trees and bushes, alive and dead, were everywhere. The fountain, like a huge, broken soup bowl, lay on the ground in two equal pieces. The roof over the monks' walk was sagging and full of holes, and there was a big bush pushing up the stones in the corridor to the next building.

She had never believed that ghosts hurt people, not even when she was a little child. She liked them and always wanted to see one. Now she thought of the monks walking around the garden in their black robes, reading and saying their prayers, and she half believed that the ghosts of three or four of them were still here. It made her feel protected and at home. She could almost hear the low hum of their voices. She crossed herself as a gust of wind blew snow off the trees, and went to the corridor that led to the hospital.

At the end of the corridor were storerooms and washing rooms and a large kitchen. In the center of the kitchen floor was a trapdoor leading down to the cellar. She walked past the kitchen and into the hospital. Wooden bed frames hung from the walls, and the place was full of sunlight and snow. There was a large linen closet near the entrance, with a chest by the door. Laurel went over to it and lifted the lid. It was full of linen shrouds, all neatly tied in little bundles. She wasn't surprised. A monastery hospital took care of dying people, and when they were dead, the monks had to be ready to wash them and dress them.

She picked up a shroud, untied it, and held it up to herself. It reached the floor and then some, so it could be folded under the feet, and there was a wide hood. She took out her piece of steel, which was as sharp as a razor at one end, cut off the bottom, and put the shroud on. Immediately she felt warmer, especially around the ears.

Food. That was the thing to look for now. She picked up two more shrouds and put them under her arm and went into the kitchen. All the shelves were empty. She was going to have to go down into the cellar. The only animals she hated were snakes and rats. Snakes would be sleeping now, but not rats. Well, there was no help in postponing things. She bent over the trapdoor, grabbed the handle, and pulled. The door was very heavy, but once she got it up about a foot, it swung easily.

"Rats? Are you down there? I have heavy shoes you can't bite through, and I'd as soon see you dead as anything."

She took two steps, and then three more. "If the truth be known, I'd prefer to see you dead. Well, I don't want to *see* you at all. I'd prefer to *know* you're dead. Have someone come and bring me the news, 'All the rats in the Kingdom are dead and buried.' That's my ideal."

She stood halfway down. There was a strong smell of vinegar. Pickles? A soul could live on pickles for a long time.

"Vermin? I know you for what you are, and I'm twenty times taller, and I have no fear of laying you out cold."

She went down the rest of the way and stood there a minute to let her eyes become accustomed to the dim light. "I don't hear anything. That's good."

It was an extensive cellar, with a low ceiling held up by stacks of flat stones. The floor was covered with pieces of wood: barrel ends, staves, broken benches, garden stakes, and hundreds of little pegs that might have been leftovers from the building of the hospital. All of it was under a yellowish dust that looked like mustard powder.

She walked around, making wider and wider circles from the bottom of the stairs. The deeper she went, the more she had to bend over and the darker it was. Just when she was beginning to think that there was nothing to be found, she came upon two packages measuring a foot high and two feet wide. There were slats around each one, and they were wrapped in waxed cloth.

She pulled and pulled at the top one, which was stuck to the bottom one, until they tipped over together and broke apart, and then she pushed the near one end over end to the bottom of the stairs. She stood up straight, which hurt because she had been bent over for so long, and then knelt down and broke the seal at the end of the package and peeled back layers and layers of cloth until she was hit by a stink that almost knocked her down.

Two-hundred-, or three-hundred-, year-old salted fish. It smelled worse than anything she had ever smelled in her whole life. Was it glowing? Nobody had ever told her not to eat food that glowed, but she was sure it wasn't a good idea. She grabbed a handful of it and went behind the stairs where it was dark, closed her eyes for a minute, and then opened them. No, it wasn't glowing. She went back to the package, tore off a piece of waxed cloth to put the fish on, and went back to the room.

8

LAUREL PUT THE FISH, an armful of wood, and the two shrouds on the floor in front of the door. "Mistress Alice?"

"Laurel?"

"I'm going to slide the bolt and come in now."

"It's only you?"

"All alone."

She opened the door. Alice was standing next to the hearth. "The fire went out," she said. "I put too much on it at one time. There was so much smoke I thought the room was catching fire. Silly. You must never leave me alone again."

Laurel went over to the fire, cleared it, and blew it back up.

"I thought you might be hurt," Alice said. "I was just making plans to climb out and come after you. I became quite distracted. What is that you're wearing?"

"A shroud. I found a chest of them in the hospital. I should have come back sooner, I know."

"It smells odd."

"That's salt fish. I should have washed my hands. The great thing is that we needn't starve. It smells terrible and it will taste awful, but there's nothing for it. We won't have to eat it forever."

Alice turned her eyes toward the open door. "Is it safe?"

"Yes, mistress. There's no one else here."

Alice smiled and went out the door and turned right toward the entrance. Laurel followed her, stopping to look in the room where she had thrown her cloak and satchel. They were still there. She picked up the cloak and, when they got to the monastery entrance, asked Alice to put it on. "It's not new. It must be fifty years old, but it's better than that blanket for keeping warm."

"Should I, do you think?"

"I can put on a second shroud, if need be. Or more. Please?"

Alice put it on. They stood next to the long trail of snow that had blown through the door, looking out toward the woods.

"I have eaten trout," Alice said after a long time. "Fresh trout is very tasty. I believe my father liked it best poached. That's a way of cooking or spicing, I'm not sure. And smoked eel can be very tasty in the afternoon with buttered bread."

"I'm sure," Laurel said.

Alice pointed. "Is that a little dent there, in the snow, where the horses tromped around waiting? There was an awful wind. No one would dare to deny that. It makes you think of the wilderness of Canada. Pictures of it, that is."

Laurel turned and walked into the chapel. There

were no benches or pews or chairs to sit on, just an empty room with an altar rail in the front and a stone tablet against the inside wall with the name of the family that had given it to the glory of God. Alice came in after her.

"Do you think we will die?"

"Certainly not, mistress. No. Nothing could be less likely. We have fire, we have water, we have food. We've escaped. Would God let us have all that, just to snatch our lives away from us, after all? Not likely."

"My aunt used to tell me stories at bedtime about good children who took to their beds with consumptions and fevers and such, and were glad to die. They would go singing hymns. I don't know very many hymns. I should."

"You'll have a long life to learn them. Now our task is to find a place to hide when he comes back for us."

"Will he come back, do you think?"

"Yes. After he gives us enough time. As he sees it, we have no fire, and nothing but our dresses to wear, and one shawl between us, and no way out, so he has every hope of our freezing soon. We must have a safe hole by tomorrow. Nothing else will do."

They left the chapel and looked around the entrance. An iron ladder ran up the wall next to the door to a trapdoor in the ceiling. "The tower," Laurel said. "If we can lock it or wedge it shut, and make him believe that we have gone away, we can wait until he leaves and follow his tracks."

She pulled on the bottom rung to make sure it was solid. "We must hide there without leaving any signs below."

Alice looked up. "There must be bells. You could go up now and ring them and people would hear us and come."

"What if he's the only one to hear them? He'll know where we are. We can't make a sound until he's come and gone."

"Oh. Yes. Of course. When I'm Harold Pomfret-Watkin's wife, I will never let anyone lock me in anywhere, ever, not even dear Harold. And I will never lock my children in anywhere, not even when I am with them."

They walked out into the snow in front of the tower and turned and looked at it.

"I could watch through the slits," Laurel said.

Alice touched her arm. "Turn and turn about? I must do my part as well as you."

"Good."

Alice smiled. "Now what must we do?"

"We'll go to the garden and eat something."

Two minutes later they were sitting on a bench in the sun, with the piece of fish between them. Neither of them was looking at it, though Laurel could see, out of the corner of her eye, the salt glinting in the sun. "Even spoiled food won't hurt you, most of the time," she said. "Granny Piersall would sometimes cook up too much food and it would sit in the kitchen window. After the third day, or the fourth, even in the winter, it would begin to turn, but she wouldn't notice because her eyes and nose were not of the best, and we would eat it. I didn't like it at all, but it never hurt me or made me sick, and it satisfied my hunger. Food would change to another color, and sometimes even change again, before we finished it. Sometimes I would tell myself that it was a spice. Shall I take the first bite?"

Alice didn't answer.

Laurel looked down at the fish sparkling and stinking in the sun. "I'll sprinkle some snow on it, which is something they do in London, not with fish but with raspberries. Father Simpson told me about it more than once."

She broke off a piece about as big as the end of her thumb, scooped a little cap of snow on top of it, and put it in her mouth and began to chew. It felt as if a needle were being driven up through the top of her mouth and into her nose. Her eyes became bleary and she turned her head away. The salt made a loud crunching sound in her ears. The snow was gone and her mouth felt dry. She forced herself to swallow, and then shut her teeth and took a deep breath, and then another. The chief thing was not to throw up. She told her stomach that there was nothing wrong, that it should welcome what it was getting and keep it.

After a minute, she turned to Alice. "It has a very fishy taste. It may not have been cooked, just laid up the way it was packed, a layer of fish, a layer of salt, a layer of fish. Some of the Saints of the Church have eaten all manner of raw things. I believe I will take five more bites. That will make a half dozen, which is a good beginning. People in the South Seas live on nothing but fish from the briny sea and coconuts their whole lives long."

She did her five more bites, and after the fifth one she made a large snowball and ate it. Her teeth throbbed from the cold, and her lips burned from the salt. "I believe I feel stronger already," she said.

"Truly?"

"Oh, yes, I'm sure I do." She stood up. "The fish is not what anyone would choose to eat. By no means. It tastes awful, if the truth be told, but it's strengthening all the same, which is the chief thing. Now you must have some. The snow helps."

"I'll eat a little if you don't watch me," Alice said. "Go back to the ladder, and wait for me. I promise I'll eat six whole bites. Then we'll climb up into the tower and see."

Laurel doubted that she would do it, but she left and went back to the entrance, and a few minutes later Alice joined her there. "Now I can tell my children that I once ate something that not even a sailor would eat."

Laurel climbed the ladder to the tower trapdoor. There was no bolt, only a rusted latch with the striker frozen open. She pushed up against the door, and a cloud of dust and snowflakes filled the air.

"Are you all right?" Alice asked.

"Yes, yes. There are some bells here, but they've fallen down from above. I'm going to go up to the top story and look about."

She climbed a second ladder and came to a room where the roof had fallen in. The floor was covered with slates and rotten wood. She went to the narrow, high front windows and looked out. Snowfields stretched a half a mile or more to the woods. She tried to find a gap at the edge of the field that would be the sign of a road or a track. After a minute, she noticed a space between some ash trees and a cluster of oaks. "You have to give the devil his due," she said quietly.

She went to the windows on the right. The meadow fell away twice in that direction, and then there was a narrow line of trees. "There must be a river," she said softly. "I must make some tracks so he'll think we went down there and fell in."

"Laurel?"

Laurel looked down into the lower room. Alice was halfway in, her feet still on the ladder, afraid to go forward or back. Laurel hurried down, grabbed her hands, and pulled her up.

"Thank you. May I ask you something I've been thinking about?"

"Of course, mistress."

"Servants, no question of being friends, do they ever call their masters or mistresses by their Christian names?"

"I don't believe so, mistress."

"If they are alone together for a long time, with their lives in danger, and they know no one will ever find out?"

"I don't know, mistress."

Alice nodded her head. "I was wondering."

They were silent for a minute. Laurel went to the right side of the tower. "We must make your uncle believe we are dead," she said. "That line of trees? There must be a river there. I will walk down to it, making a trail of footprints, tramp around near the water, and come back walking backward, so there will be two sets of footprints, both going that way, and he'll think we escaped and went there and drowned."

Alice held up her finger. "Or, another scheme, we

could gather a basket of stones, and carry it up here, and as he walks through the door pour them on his head, and then we run down and get in the carriage and drive to my Intended."

"Well," Laurel said, "we could do that, if we could find a basket. But the stones are all under the snow, and hard to dig, and we might miss him."

Alice put up her finger again. "But still we could catch him. If we missed him with the stones, we could have a pot of hot coals waiting, and when he pushed up the trapdoor and started to climb in, pour them on his head. Do you know how to make charcoal?"

"Oh, yes. But your aunt might be in the carriage. Or, if he saw us, instead of coming up he might nail the trapdoor shut or set fire to the tower. Besides which, mistress, do you really want to kill him, no matter how?"

Alice looked down. "I don't know."

"If we can escape without it," Laurel said, "I think we must try. Still, I'll go and begin making charcoal, to keep us warm while we hide."

"You have the best ideas always," Alice said.

Laurel shook her head. "No, I don't. You simply haven't had a chance to see me a fool yet."

9

IN THE MIDDLE OF THE AFTERNOON, Laurel went out the door of the monastery and started walking toward the river. The sun was halfway down in the sky, and it was turning colder, but there was still plenty of time to get to the river and tramp around and come back.

Alice was in the room napping, after watching Laurel make charcoal for a few hours.

When she got to the first slope, Laurel stopped and washed her hands in the snow and dried them on her dirty shroud. They still smelled of fish. There were crows squawking in the trees. One of them came flapping out over the field and made a big circle and flew back into the woods again. Then another flew out and circled around her. She held out her arm and told him to come down for a visit, but he pretended not to know what she was talking about.

She started down the slope. The grass underneath the snow was very slippery, so she went slowly. When she got to the bottom, she heard Alice calling her name.

She turned around and looked back up the hill. Alice

was standing there, her breath making puffs of steam in the air.

"Laurel?"

"It's slippery. You must be careful coming down. There's no hurry."

Alice came slowly down the hill. She was crying. When she was almost to the bottom, she stopped. "Why did you go?"

"I beg your pardon. You were fast asleep. I thought you knew."

"What will happen to me? You must never leave me alone. Never."

Laurel went to her. "I ask your pardon, mistress. I will never do it again. I promise."

Alice looked down and closed her eyes. "Kiss me?"

Laurel put her arms around her and kissed her. "Everything will come out right," she said. "Life is supposed to be hard sometimes. It's planned that way, to make us strong. It will all come out right."

They stood in each other's arms for a long while, listening to the crows call back and forth in the trees. Finally, Laurel let her go. "We must try to make two clear tracks, and we'll walk backward in them when we're done. It will be easy."

They started off, with Alice to the left and a step or two behind. "Will you bear witness to my children? When they ask you if I really did these things, eating raw fish and climbing into towers and wearing your old cloak, will you tell them it's true?"

"They'll believe you, mistress."

"No, they won't. Not if I have nothing but boys. Boys can be great doubters. You and I will keep it a secret until the youngest reaches a certain age, lest they have bad dreams thinking about it. Of course, I could just go on having baby after baby, and then one would always be too young. Do you think that's a wicked idea?"

"No, mistress, not at all."

"Then I won't repent of it."

They went down the second slope and stopped at the trees. Below them, they could see the river. Laurel looked at Alice. "Do you want to go with me down to the shore?"

"Yes."

"I'll lead."

Laurel took her hand, and they stepped down onto a stone ledge. At the end of the ledge was a bush covered with small brown leaves. They worked their way around the bush and down onto a snow-covered tree trunk that was too slippery to stay on. Laurel jumped off first, and helped Alice down. They went down a steep slope covered with small stones, and then across a rotten tree trunk.

"We're halfway," Alice said, and they stopped and looked at the river and the shore. Everything on the riverbank was covered with a coat of clear, smooth ice.

Laurel turned to Alice. "No use both of us slipping and sliding around down there. I can leave tracks enough for two."

"No please, I want to go, too."

"As long as you're careful. We'll cross over to that level place and go down from there." Laurel turned, and as she reached out to take hold of a branch, her left foot went out from under her, she fell hard on her side, and began bouncing toward the water. She grabbed for a small tree, missed it, hit a rock, twisted around, rolled across the bank, and slammed into a tree that was half in the water and half out.

"I'm all right, I'm all right," she yelled. "Don't come down."

But Alice was already on her way. "I'll help you. Don't let go."

"Go slowly. Be careful." Laurel looked down. Her left leg was in the water, her hands were cut and bleeding, and her right knee had little stones and bits of moss stuck in it.

Alice knelt down next to her. "Are you truly all right?"

"I fell."

"You have your leg in the water."

"I know."

"Can you pull it out and get up? Shall I help?"

Alice put her hands under Laurel's arms and helped her to stand up.

"I'm quite whole," Laurel said. "Just wet." She looked around. "I think we've left enough tracks and mess. We must walk in our old footprints."

They backed up the bank until they got to the ledge they had started on, and then stopped and looked down. "It's a ghastly sight, isn't it?" Alice said. "Two young women trying to find their way across and drowning? You tore a bit from your dress. Do you see it? On the bottom branch of that little tree next to the mound."

Laurel couldn't see it. Suddenly she felt very cold.

"Are you shivering?"

"Only a little. I think, instead of walking backward,

as long as we stay in our old tracks, he won't see the difference."

So they started back, Alice stepping carefully in Laurel's tracks, and Laurel in Alice's. "May I ask you a very serious question?" Alice said when they got to the top of the first slope. "What would have happened to us if we had fallen in? One right after the other, into the river—carried away? It would have happened in a flash. One moment safe, the next in that freezing cold water."

"I would have tried to get you ashore."

Alice shook her head. "But, no matter how brave you were, no matter how strong, you would never have been able to do it. We would have been carried away."

"I suppose so."

"Drowned. It would all have been over within the blink of an eye. What I wonder is, what would our prospects have been?"

"We would have died."

"And then?"

"We would have been washed out to sea, unless we got snagged on something or our clothes pulled us down or there was a sudden freeze."

"And then? Speaking of our souls?"

"An angel would have come and taken us away."

"That's what I think, too. And after that? Aunt Salvia was in Paris once. She told me they sold pictures of hell on street corners, with the fires burning, and the inmates in torment, unclothed, still doing their mortal sins through all eternity, but getting no pleasure out of them. Is that what you think happens to bad people?"

"I don't know, mistress. It might be."

"So Uncle Percy, if he went there, would smoke horrible cigars and say cruel things back and forth with Aunt Salvia, and plot murder forever and ever, in misery?"

"Father Simpson used to warn people about seeing others in hell," Laurel said. "God is ready to accept a timely and sincere repentance before the moment of death, he would say."

Alice nodded her head. "I suppose He has to. Are we walking too slowly? Your lips are blue. We have to dry your clothes the moment we get in the room."

"Don't hurry," Laurel said. "You'll spoil the footprints."

They walked the rest of the way to the monastery in silence, and as soon as she got dry, Laurel sat on the hearth and began making charcoal. She worked late into the night, eating bits of fish with snow every once in a while. Then they fetched another bed in, and went to sleep.

The next morning, very early, they got up and carried loads of charcoal to the tower, cleaned the hearth, went up the ladder, and locked themselves in to wait for Lord Stayne.

"Is it getting very very cold," Alice asked, "or is it just my weakness that makes it seem so?"

"No, mistress, you can believe it. I've never felt colder myself."

Lord Stayne didn't come all day, and the charcoal ran out before dark, and Laurel spent most of the night making more. By sunrise they were tired and hungry and thirsty, but they had enough charcoal to carry them through another day or more. About ten o'clock, when the tower room was half in sun, half in shadow, Lord and Lady Stayne appeared in a wagon.

Alice looked at them coming across the field, and shut her eyes. "I don't want to see them."

Laurel turned and smiled at her. "There's no need."

"When they get close, you must make sure I stay still and don't jump up and wave. You must be ready to sit right on me. I don't trust myself."

"If you want me to."

"Yes, please."

Laurel watched the wagon through the window slats as it came closer and closer. Lady Stayne was in her long fur coat with the white collar, and Lord Stayne was wearing his long coat and a fur hat. In the back of the wagon, tied down on boards, were two coffins, one shiny and black, the other dull and yellow.

"I shan't be able to pour coals on him," Alice whispered. "That was all just boasting. Look, my hands are shaking."

"There's no need. They won't find us," Laurel said.

"I couldn't stamp on his fingers, either."

Still watching them, Laurel put her finger over her mouth. "Shhhhh."

Suddenly, Lady Stayne yelled, "Stop! Look! My God, they've flown." She was standing and pointing at the footprints leading to the river. "If God doesn't damn you, it's only because He's a worse fool than you are."

Lord Stayne snapped his whip and drove quickly to the entrance. He pulled up his horses and jumped down and ran inside. After a few seconds they heard him yell something, and then he came out again. "They've flown."

Lady Stayne threw the whip at him. "God's garters, man, you see their trail, go after them."

He hopped off across the field, making a path between the two lines of footprints. He fell down twice, but he got up right away both times and kept going.

Lady Stayne climbed down from the wagon and disappeared through the entrance. Laurel and Alice heard her crossing the hall, and then nothing. Had she gone into the chapel? Had she tiptoed the other way and into the corridor? Or was she standing there, directly beneath them, listening? Laurel reached into a drift of clean white snow, made two snowballs, and gave one to Alice. They nibbled their snowballs, waiting for something to happen.

After a long time they heard Lord Stayne's voice from a great distance. He was calling out something, but they couldn't tell what it was. Laurel went to the window. He was coming to the top of the first slope. He wasn't running, but he was doing his quick, hopping walk. He had the strip of cloth from Laurel's dress stretched between his hands, and he was wrapping it first around one hand and then around the other. He stopped and yelled as loudly as he could. "Salvia? Salvia? Be of good cheer. They're dead as salt herring. Couldn't be better."

He hopped back to the wagon and looked down between the coffins, as if he expected to see her sleeping there. "Where are you, my sweet? All's well that ends well. Now, don't you hide from me, my little sphinx." He came into the monastery. Laurel and Alice heard him walk into the chapel, stop, and then walk across the entrance hall. Then there was silence.

They looked at each other. Alice's eyes were open very wide, and she was breathing fast. Laurel smiled. "It's all right."

They waited. Laurel made another snowball and offered it to Alice, but she shook her head. After a minute, they heard someone crunching through the snow near the front wall of the monastery. Laurel looked down. It was Lady Stayne, and she was carrying a table leg. She stepped behind the entrance door and waited. A long time passed, and then Lord Stayne walked out. "Salvia? Did you hear? They're dead and gone. No more games, now. Make pax."

She stepped from behind the door and swung the table leg at him. It hit him in the side of the head and he sat down on the snow. "Great God, woman, what are you trying to do?" He pushed himself backward and got up and started to run. She came right behind him, swinging the leg again and hitting him on the shoulder, knocking him down. She then jumped on him and tried to smother him, but he wriggled free and stood up and stuck his tongue out at her. "Salvia, please, show a bit of mercy. I don't know what made me do that. Let me help you up. It was a serious social error."

She got onto her hands and knees, and then stood up and threw the table leg at him. It missed. She tilted her head to the side, gasping for air. "You want me dead. You always have. But you're right, we must make peace." She walked slowly toward him, and when she was very close, she reached out and grabbed his ear and tried to bite it. They fell down and rolled over and over in the snow, grunting and gasping and squeaking like two animals trying to kill each other.

Laurel looked at Alice. She had some fish in her hand, and she was breaking off pieces of it and pushing them into her mouth as she watched her aunt and uncle fighting. Her face was the color of ashes.

After a while, Lord Stayne pulled himself away and stood up. There was blood running from his forehead and his left ear. "They're dead," he said. "They're drowned. You're trying to kill me. I insist that you cease."

She sat on the ground, her face red and covered with sweat. "You are trying to put me in my grave," she said. "I will not have you give me an untimely death. Now, help me stand up."

He helped her up, and she swung at him one more time. He swung back, hitting her on the side of her head. Her bonnet and wig flew high into the air. It looked, for a moment, as if he had knocked her head off. She stood there, her ears sticking out. She was totally hairless, except for some black fuzz running across the top of her head from ear to ear. "For shame!" she screamed. "Fetch, fetch, fetch!"

Lord Stayne went to get her wig, which had come loose from her bonnet and was lying a few feet away from it.

Laurel looked at Alice again. She was breathing fast, with her mouth slightly open. She had the helpless, frightened look on her face that people get when they're about to throw up.

Laurel shook her head.

Alice shook her head, too, her eyes very wide open.

Laurel put her right arm around Alice's shoulder and her left hand behind Alice's head and drew her against her chest, so that the sound would be muffled, and Alice vomited up the fish. She retched again and again, and Laurel kept hold of her until she was finished. Then she loosened her grip slowly, keeping her left hand on Alice's shoulder in case she had to pull her in again, dipped her free hand in a bit of snow, and put it on Alice's forehead.

Alice kept her eyes closed for a minute. She looked peaceful. Then she opened her eyes and stared at the mess she had made on Laurel's shroud. She started to say something, but Laurel put her finger in front of her mouth.

"I'm sorry," Alice whispered.

"No need." Laurel took off her top shroud and rolled it in a ball and put it aside, and then went over to the window and looked at Lord and Lady Stayne. She was sitting on the wagon box, her bonnet and hair back in place, and he was standing next to the wagon looking up at her.

"Poor little cubs," she said. "It's a dreadful shame."

Lord Stayne nodded his head. "Very sad."

"May the Lord show them every possible mercy."

"Amen, dear, dear lady."

Lady Stayne looked up at the sky. "I pray they had a few moments for repentance, but it's not likely. Must we go back to the manor with empty coffins?"

"I fear so, my dear. Their bodies are miles away by now."

"Pity. Frozen in some little pool, perhaps. You have

a small cut over your eye. Did you fall as you were searching for them?"

"I must have."

"I'll care for it at home."

He came around the front of the wagon and climbed up beside her, turned the horses, and drove away.

10

THEY WERE TOO TIRED to follow Lord and Lady Stayne's wagon tracks right away, so they stayed one more night at the monastery. When they woke up the next morning, the room was full of sunlight. Somewhere, a bird was singing. Laurel remade the fire and they stood next to it until they were almost hot. Then Laurel put on two extra shrouds, wrapped the blanket tightly around herself, put her satchel over her shoulder, and led the way out.

"Will you miss it?" Alice asked as they were crossing the field toward the trees, following the wagon tracks. "Feel homesick for the monastery?"

"I don't believe so, mistress."

"I will. It's been home to me." They stopped and turned around. "I will forever remember the tower where we watched all night and had to conceal ourselves from my murderous uncle and aunt. I've been thinking. Do you know, you're the only one in the world who knows I am who I am? Nobody else has seen me for over a year, and I have no relations, and my uncle and aunt will deny me, if it comes to that. None of that matters, in the great scheme of things. Seeing my Intended is everything to me. Should we be walking faster?"

The distance to the trees was greater than they had thought, and after a minute they slowed down again. Finally, they entered the trees. Laurel felt a little dizzy and wanted to stop, but she knew it was too soon.

"Are you all right?" Alice asked.

Laurel nodded. "Oh yes. We'll want to find a farm as soon as we can where we can get a bit of hot soup and bread, and have a place to sleep."

"You don't want to stop and rest?"

"Oh, no, not I."

A few minutes later, at the top of a small hill, they did stop. Laurel brushed off a stone for Alice to sit on, and cleared another for herself. They each ate a snowball.

"If my Intended turns me away, I will enter a religious order of nursing sisters and spend my life in the service of Church and Empire, possibly in India, though I remember Egypt fondly," Alice said.

"If we find a way to prove who you are," Laurel said, "you can go home."

"We can't. Nobody knows me. No, if my Intended disowns me, everything will end, my entire world will be a ruin. But I will be strong, and accept my fate, and not hold it against him."

They were silent for a while.

"John Frame will take us in if need be," Laurel said. "Your steward, who lives in a cave across the river?"

Alice shook her head. "No. I will become a nun. Are those railway tracks? Over that way?"

Laurel stood up and looked. The tracks were plain to see, between two small hills less than half a mile away. They both immediately felt stronger. They walked down to the tracks, looked and listened carefully, and then crossed the tracks into a grove between them and the road. Before they stepped out onto the road, Laurel groomed Alice as best she could, pulling the sticks and burrs and dead leaves from her cloak and slapping it clean. "I wish I had a brush," she said, drawing back Alice's hair and braiding it. Finally, she took a corner of the shroud in her satchel and had Alice spit on it and wiped her face.

"I believe you're thinner, mistress. I'm sure of it."

"Do I look like a stick?"

"No, mistress. Not at all."

"Or unwell? A young woman needs a robust yet tender appearance. I do wish we had a man to advise us. A man would know about train schedules, and where they went. Men know how to keep afloat."

"We should go left," Laurel said. "It's the Saltfield direction. I remember this piece of the highway. There are some little farms close to town."

They started along the road. There were a lot of frozen puddles, and Laurel slipped and almost fell down a couple of times, but she was so happy knowing where she was, and that they would soon find a place for the night, she didn't mind. "I'm not a man, but I will get you safe to your Intended," she said.

"What if he doesn't even know me, hasn't even heard of me? That could be."

Laurel nodded. "Yes."

"Have you been thinking that, too?"

"Mistress, I will not talk of this any longer. Now we must think of a bed for tonight, and food. We are alive and rich. I have seven shillings in my money pouch. We're better off than any number of people on the road, some of them sick and starving."

"You're right, I know you are," Alice said. "I'm a great bother, aren't I?"

"Not at all, mistress."

Alice stopped and put her hand on Laurel's arm. "Then, may we go to Saltfield station first and find out about trains to Hobson, and then find a place for the night? Please?"

Laurel thought for a moment. "Yes, but we must try to walk a bit faster."

When they came into Saltfield, they went directly to the railway station, a big brick building with a dome roof and stone pillars, standing at the end of a long, narrow park. The stairs had rope carpets on them so that people wouldn't slip, and the doorknobs were brass lions' heads.

They went to the ticket stall and Laurel asked for two third-class tickets to Hobson. The ticket seller asked them if they wanted return tickets, which would be cheaper still, but Alice leaned in and said no, that the people they were going to see were certain to take them in.

As Laurel was counting her change, Alice tugged at her sleeve and pointed to an old lady standing by the entrance to the platforms selling boiled eggs, two for a penny. "Do you think?" she said. "The price needn't worry us. I'll soon be richer than anyone could imagine."

Laurel looked at her. "We'll buy four," she said. "But we must sit down and eat them very slowly, and take five minutes by the clock between them."

They went to the lady and bought the eggs, which came with a little paper of salt, and went to the corner by the big coal stove and sat down. "Mustn't wolf it," Laurel said.

"I know," Alice said. "Ladies must never appear hungry."

They took their time for the sake of their stomachs and because it felt so good sitting next to the stove and watching the people going by. When they were finished, and Laurel had thrown away the shells, Alice asked if they could have just one more apiece. "We can afford it," she said, "and they were quite small eggs, after all."

Laurel shook her head. "Please, mistress, we cannot spend a farthing more until we know our prospects. We don't yet have a bed for the night. We must arrange that before anything else."

They crossed the waiting room side by side, went out the main door, down the stairs, and into the long, narrow park that led from the station to the highroad. On the way, Laurel asked Alice to forgive her for not buying the third egg. "You needn't beg my pardon," Alice said. "You always know best."

When they were halfway through the park, a high, black four-horse carriage came turning out of a side street, hit the corner curb with an awful crack, and knocked over an ashcan, sending it spinning into the front of a building. Sitting in the carriage was Lord Stayne, wearing a gray coat with a black collar, his left eye black and swollen, and bandages on his forehead and his ear. He was hanging on to a strap over the window and trying to light a cigar with one hand.

Laurel's heart gave an awful thump and started pounding. Alice turned suddenly pale. "Oh, God save us," she said. Laurel put her arms around her and held her until the carriage had turned right at the end of the street.

"It's safe. He didn't see us. You have nothing to worry about. Take a deep breath. Let it out. Good. Now take another. And another. Good."

Holding on to her arm, Laurel led her across the street and into a bakery shop. The windows were steamed up, and the baker was pulling raisin cakes out of the oven with a long wooden paddle. Laurel sat Alice down on a bench near the door and went and asked for a twopenny loaf that wasn't still hot, because Granny Piersall had taught her never to eat bread straight out of the oven. She paid for it, broke off a piece, and gave it to Alice to eat. "Sit right here. No hurry. They don't mind."

After a minute, Alice stood up and told Laurel she felt fine, and they went out onto the street and started walking again. "We're lucky," Laurel said as they turned left onto the highroad. "He's going in the other direction, getting farther and farther away with every moment. Eat a bit more bread."

They kept walking fast until they had crossed the bridge going out of town. There was a mill at the end of it, its water wheel frozen solid.

"Is this the river we drowned in?" Alice asked.

Laurel thought for a moment. "It could be, mistress.

Now we must look for a place for the night. We'll know the right place when we see it. God will show it to us."

"Do you know about the snakes in India that can freeze you?" Alice asked.

"No, mistress."

"There are snakes in India that can freeze you just by looking you in the eye. You may try to move, but there you are, you can't, and then he just creeps up to you and bites you in the ankle and you fall down dead. Aunt Salvia could do that to me as quick as a wink. That's why I'd never dare see her again. Or my uncle."

After walking half an hour, they came to a dairy farm with a small house and a good-sized barn. A woman stood in the kitchen door, with an apron full of onions. She picked one out, and then another, and walked over to the compost heap and dropped them on top. Alice and Laurel turned in at the gate. Suddenly Alice started walking faster.

"Good day," she said.

"Good day."

"I know we appear dreadful in every respect, but we are merely two young innocents seeking a place to spend the night. We have a little money, but we would prefer not to have to pay anything. We are ready to work."

The woman gathered the ends of her apron in her left hand and waved to her daughters, who were coming around the barn, to go back to work. "Gypsies?"

Alice shook her head. "Heavens, no. We are quite far away from our home, and do not wish to be on the road after nightfall."

The woman looked at Laurel's shrouds, cut off at the

bottom, which hung down between the end of the blanket and her ankles. "You travel in that?"

"We take the train early tomorrow morning," Alice said. "We are not unsavory young women, not in the least. If I may explain? This is my first time making such a request. We have run away from home, where we are hated. I am soon to be married. My Intended is very rich and powerful, and he will see to it that everyone who helps me is rewarded. Meanwhile, to show our goodness of heart, we are ready to labor to repay your generosity."

The woman nodded her head. "A pretty speech."

Alice smiled. "Thank you very much. I composed it between the railway station and here. This is the first time out loud."

"I will thank you to keep it to yourself and away from my daughters. They hear more than enough to turn their heads as it is. We are Christians. We know what we must do for the poor on our doorstep. My younger child, Eleanor, can sleep between the two of you on the wide bed. Rowena will come in with me. I have a ditch wanting clearing. After that, you can shovel the cow stalls."

"Thank you," Alice said. "We're ready to labor until sundown and beyond."

"I'm sure that's very good of you."

They went to work. Teatime was a cup of milk. Alice had never held a shovel before, and she couldn't get the trick of sliding her left hand down to the scoop end, so she was forever spilling what she picked up. She got terrible blisters, but she didn't complain.

When it was dark, Eleanor and Rowena came into

the barn to do the milking. While they milked, they told the latest gossip. A young woman of good family named Alice Plunderfield, they said, had been murdered. There were two stories about what had happened to her. One was that she had been strangled by her Irish personal maid, after being carried away through the night to an old monastery, forced to submit to Satanic ceremonies, and taken to the river for a Satanic baptism. The other story was that her maid was an Irish atheist who knew the secrets of magnetism, and had put her under a magnetic cloud and drawn her into the river by means of a lightning rod.

Eleanor believed in the Satanic ceremony story, but Rowena was sure the magnetism story was true because she had once seen a lightning rod at a fair and knew how powerful electricity was. "It can make your hair stand on end, truly," she said, "and when it gets in the hands of wicked people, no one for miles around is safe. You mustn't tell Mama we told you. She knows nothing of the world."

They ate a big dinner and went straight to bed. They were very tired, the big bed was soft and warm, and they slept without moving all night long. Breakfast was gruel with bits of apple in it, and milk.

They were back at the railway station in plenty of time to catch the 7:30 train. It was delayed twice on the way to Hobson, because of ice in the switches, but still the trip took only an hour and a half. "It would have taken me more than a day to walk this," Laurel said as they got down in the Hobson station. "It takes your breath away."

The Pomfret-Watkin estate took up most of the west

side of the town. A high brick wall with spikes on top ran all the way around it, and there was a wide iron gate. Laurel and Alice stood at the gate for a long time, looking up the hill toward the house. The estate was like a park, with little groves of trees by the road, and benches, and circles of rosebushes.

Alice took her paper doll from the bosom of her dress. "This is my greatest treasure," she said. It had been bent in half, and the right leg was torn at the knee. "I was unfair to him," Alice said. "Why did I ever tell you that his hands were stumpy? They're perfect."

"He's very handsome, mistress."

"Is my face clean?"

Laurel looked her over carefully. "You look beautiful."

"Good. Of course, true men and good see your heart, and the rest doesn't matter to them."

She kissed the doll and then tore it into tiny pieces and handed them to Laurel. "Dolls are for little girls. Now I must become a woman. I think, for a man, the most important gift is a good mother. If a man is brought up by a good mother, in a beautiful home like this, with paintings and statues and fine music and books, he must become a wonder when he grows up."

Laurel looked down and said nothing.

"I memorized a sonnet for just this hour," Alice said, "so that if everything else flew out of my mind I would have something to say to him as we stood together on the balcony or in the garden. It was by Elizabeth Barrett Browning. It had a bird in it somewhere."

"Mistress, shall we go to the house?"

"My legs won't move. They're frozen. I can't even feel them."

"He might be watching you right now from one of those high windows, and wondering why we don't come."

"Do you think he might be?"

"He might."

"My mouth is dry. I believe I need some water."

Laurel reached up and broke an icicle off the gate. The snap of it made Alice jump, and she started walking toward the house very fast. "We must simply walk up to the front door and announce ourselves," she said. "We were called to be here. No person of decency could turn us away, not and live with himself in peace. We need only to keep our dignity. Aren't the trees ancient and lovely?"

They fell silent. The only sound was the sound of their shoes on the hard-packed snow. The house was like a palace. Laurel's heart started beating fast. She was sure that they were going to be sent away again, probably with rude remarks, and then what would she do with Alice?

The cobblestone circle in front of the house was as big as a racing course. It had been swept entirely clear of snow, and it was completely dry. A wagon piled high with barrels drove around the corner of the house and crossed the circle, the sound of its wheels echoing against the front wall. They stepped aside, and it rolled on toward the front gate.

"We must go the rest of the way with dignity," Alice said. "We belong here more than anywhere else, that's certain. They'll have a solid brass knocker, I'm sure."

"I should think so, mistress."

"Did you ever see so many windows?"

"Never in my life."

A maid in a long gray dress and a white apron and cap came out a side door and walked toward the carriage house. When she was almost there, a man in a black uniform came out and met her and they stood talking. A second maid, who looked about fifteen years old, ran out and joined them. After listening a minute, she whispered something in the first maid's ear and took hold of her hand and started pulling her away. Both of them were giggling now, the one who wanted to stay and the one who wanted to go, and they swung slowly around in a circle and then ran back inside.

Laurel and Alice crossed the cobblestone circle and went up the three marble steps to the front door.

"It is brass," Alice said.

Laurel took a deep breath, lifted the knocker, and let it fall. It made a loud bang, and there seemed to be an echo inside the house. Laurel picked it up and let it fall again, and then they waited. They heard somebody walking along the front of the house toward them, but they didn't even look that way.

The door opened. An old man in a formal suit looked down at them. "We have something for you in the kitchen." He pointed toward the left side of the house. "Second door."

Laurel put her hands behind her back. "We are not what we seem, sir. We are here to speak with Mr. Harold Pomfret-Watkin. We are not wanderers. I am a servant, and this lady is Quality."

The old man kept pointing. "The family receives visitors by invitation or by appointment. Such business as we have with your sort is carried on at the kitchen door. The family takes a direct part in the distribution of charity only on Christmas Day."

"Please," Alice said. "The master of the house will know my name, I am sure."

The man put down his hand. "If the generosity of the Pomfret-Watkin family is not to your liking, we must see you to the road."

Laurel took half a step forward. "Sir, this woman has been told by her aunt and uncle, both educated people, that she is betrothed to Mr. Harold Pomfret-Watkin. It may be so, and it may not be so, but it is your duty, I believe, to tell him that she has arrived as promised. Please."

The butler looked behind them. They turned. A footman in a red uniform was standing on the bottom step.

Laurel looked back at the butler. "It is my mistress's life."

He thought for a minute. "We do not expect any visitors until noon, so you are not encumbering the entrance. I will see after this."

"Thank you."

He closed the door. The footman came up another step. They stood in silence for a long while, watching the door. It opened, and the butler stuck his head out. "Jack, see that they find the gate." The door slammed shut.

The footman grabbed them, pulled them backward down the stairs, and started walking them across the circle. His grip was very hard, and he took long steps. When they were halfway to the gate, he let them go and took a few steps back. "You stink."

They didn't answer.

"Like rotten fish. Go on. I'll be standing right here watching you. If you slow down or look back, I'll be on you with dogs."

They walked on quickly, and when they got close to the high iron gate, they heard a horse galloping behind them. Laurel pulled Alice to the side of the road, and the horse and rider flew by them and out the gate and then wheeled around and came back. It was Harold Pomfret-Watkin. He had grown a mustache, and his face was a little more round than the one in the picture, and he looked taller. He had beautiful blue eyes. Laurel looked at his hands. They were stumpy.

He smiled down on them. He was wearing a brown wool daytime suit with a black cape pulled over it, and ordinary walking shoes. He didn't have a hat, and his hair was in a tangle. "Good day," he said.

Alice nodded and Laurel curtsied. They said "Good day" in return.

"I intend you no harm. Perish the thought." He leaned forward and patted his horse's neck. "Lest you think, for example, that I am keeping you here while my man rides out the side gate to fetch the constable, I assure you that you need have no such fear. I would never deceive anyone, especially young women. I have my code. So, now, we're clear on that score. Isn't that good? Clear the air? Now you must have a turn to have your say."

He smiled. He had long eyelashes, and his cheeks were red.

"Yes? No? Nothing to say, for the nonce?" He looked at Laurel. "You admire my horse?"

"Yes. He's very well trained, sir."

"Indeed. Indeed. Absolutely."

"The bit may be drawn too tight. See the way he turns his head to the left?"

"No. Not possible. I put it in myself."

He took his right foot out of the stirrup and crossed it over his left, as if he were sitting on a sofa instead of a horse. "When Mr. Harrison, our faithful butler, told me you were here, I was in the midst of reading Shelley's dramatic poem "Prometheus Unbound," where he writes, '*Our task is done, / We are free to dive, or soar, or run*; / *Beyond or around, / Or within the bound, / Which clips the world with darkness round.*' Do you know it? Well, perhaps not. At any rate, I was giving Shelley my complete attention. Mr. Harrison was already gone before I understood clearly what he had been telling me. Hence the scratch costume you see me in. May I ask? What led you to attempt your fraud here, on me? I must tell you, it is not flattering in the least. It is, in fact, somewhat insulting."

"We did not intend to insult you, sir," Laurel said. "My mistress came here telling you the truth as she knew it."

Harold Pomfret-Watkin sat up straighter. "Oh, no. Did I say insulting? That's not the word I want at all. Goodness me. I don't feel in the least insulted. By two young women in off the road? How could I be?"

"My mistress would never ask anything unless she believed she had a right to it."

He put his hands on his chest and smiled, showing all his teeth. "My hand in marriage? Isn't that, well, rather much?"

"We were misled by wicked persons."

Alice looked up at him for a moment. "We truly beg your pardon."

He kept his eyes on Laurel. "It was quite ridiculous, indeed, to think that I would allow myself to become engaged to a person I had never seen, social station quite aside. Entirely aside. I mean to say, with me, any hoax of this sort was bound to fail. In fact, if you must know, a bridal candidate is coming here this afternoon. I won't accept her, but her parents are old family friends, so she deserves a try at winning my heart, don't you think? Do I know your name?"

Laurel turned to Alice. "May I present Mistress Alice Plunderell of Plunderell Manor, Saltfield."

"And you are?"

"Laurel Bybank, sir."

"I see. Quite. Well, as you have discovered, I am mad about Shelley, but I am also a great admirer of the poet Byron. Bravery, passion, cunning of the animal sort, all move my heart, as they did his." He raised his finger in the air. "However, as the Apostle St. Paul said, we must not only be as wise as serpents, we must also be as innocent as doves. Yes? Your action lacked the dovelike quality, wouldn't you agree? But let us put all that behind us." He reached into his pocket. "May I offer you this?"

He held out a small leather bag tied with a yellow string.

Laurel looked at Alice. "Thank you, no, sir." And they both started walking toward the gate.

Harold Pomfret-Watkin turned his horse and came along beside them. "It's an entire ten shillings. You could use part of it to purchase a copy of the Scriptures to study. There are wonderful Bibles being printed these days, some with very attractive tinted pictures. They make it all seem quite real."

Laurel and Alice went out through the gate and turned left and walked along the high wall in the direction of the railway station. When they came to the corner, Alice went around it and stopped and started to shake. "Oh, Laurel," she said, "he has killed me."

Laurel put her arms around her. "I'll see after you, mistress."

"It was proper not to take the money."

"Absolutely."

"He has killed me."

Laurel shook her head. "I'll take care of you, mistress. We'll make our way. We have friends."

After a minute Laurel stepped back, keeping her hands on Alice's shoulders. "We'll take the train back to Saltfield."

Alice took a deep breath and wiped her eyes with the back of her hand. "Laurel? Have you ever loved a man to distraction?"

"I'm too young, mistress."

"He was beautiful. A thousand times more than his picture. So tall."

"It was a tall horse, mistress."

"Now I know what I must do. I must wait a few days, and then come back here and enter his service, in the humblest, lowliest job, and spend the rest of my life near him, and never tell him who I am until I reach my deathbed. He will come and kneel down to hear me whisper his name. And I will spend all my free time reading Shelley and the Bible. As St. Paul said, I will be as innocent as a dove."

"He was wrong about that."

"Pardon?"

"Mr. Pomfret-Watkin was wrong about who said we should be wise as serpents and innocent as doves. It was Jesus, in the Gospel of St. Matthew. I think, when we get back to the railway station, I will write him and tell him."

11

THE TRAIN FROM HOBSON was very cold, and when it got to Saltfield, Laurel and Alice hurried across the platform and went into the waiting room and sat down next to the stove. The clock over the entrance said 11:30. After they had stopped shivering, Laurel asked Alice if she wanted an egg from the egg lady. Alice shook her head. "I must become accustomed to hardship and not having my own way," she said.

Laurel reached out and touched her arm. "You've already had hardship enough for one day."

"No, I don't believe so. I will stay here and get a little warmer, and then we will find John Frame's cave. He'll be there, won't he? You're sure of that?"

"I know he's faithful, and there's a whole wall of food there."

"I will rest a few days, and then go back to my Harold."

They sat in silence a while, watching the people come and go. Just as they were getting up to leave, Mr. Lloyd walked into the station. Laurel turned her back to him.

"Mistress? Do you see the man in black who just came in? He has the silk mourner's fan in his lapel? That's Mr. Lloyd, your uncle's steward. Do you see him?"

"Yes."

"Don't stare. What's he doing?"

"He's going toward the stationmaster's office. Now he's there. He's knocking on the door. He's waiting, tapping his foot. The stationmaster has opened the door. They're talking. Now he's coming out and they're going over to the notice board. Mr. Lloyd is giving him a paper, and he's tacking it up. It has a black border and some pictures on it. They're shaking hands."

"Is he leaving?"

"Not yet. Yes. Now he's going. He just went out the door."

They waited a minute, and then walked to the board. The paper was Alice's funeral notice. It had a picture of an angel on the left side, and a willow tree on the right.

GOD CALLS HIS DEAREST CHILDREN HOME!

A Grieving Borough Mourns

ALICE ELIZABETH ANNE PLUNDERELL

St. John's Church
5 January, Noon

Alice put her finger on the funeral notice and ran it back and forth over her name. "Perhaps I ought to have an egg, after all. Do you think?"

Laurel went and bought four eggs, and they returned to the corner by the stove and ate them. "Laurel?" Alice said after they had been sitting together in silence. "I sometimes think about my funeral. Do you ever? I know it's sinful to brood on such things, but someone could find herself thinking about it without any great harm, don't you think? Wondering what it would be like? Have you ever done that?"

"Yes. Once in a while."

"Then I'm not that odd, do you think? When I think about it, it's always the same. I'm floating up in the air over the altar. I haven't seen St. John's since I was a child, before my parents took me to Egypt. Even then it seemed ever so small to me, just a chapel, really. And there are lots and lots of people, crowded inside and all over the lawn, and I can see them all, as if I could look right through the stone walls, and they're all whispering to each other, and wiping away tears from their eyes, and saying how wonderful I was, and similar things. They're all wearing black, even the poorest ones, and I feel like an orphan again, the way I did after Mommy and Daddy died, except now it's all right, because everyone everywhere loves me. It's all vanity, of course, nothing could be more so, but it's sweet, too, in a fashion. Do you think it would be wrong if I went? Do you think God might be angry with me, as if I were mocking a holy occasion?"

Laurel shook her head. "Not at all, mistress."

"We won't have to go into the chapel unless we want to. Naturally, it won't be at all like my dream. No one really truly loves me or cares. I've prepared myself for that."

"That's not true, mistress. There are many people who love you. Mr. Regius, your stablemaster, would do anything for you. So would I. So would John Frame. And there are people I don't know at all, servants your aunt and uncle drove away from the house, who would like nothing better than to come back into your service."

Alice took hold of Laurel's hand. "Do you know, if I were to die today, and go to heaven, my best memories of life in this world would be my memories of what we did, and I would pray for you more than for anyone else."

"Thank you, mistress."

"The finest thing about becoming a servant, as I plan to do, is that then we will occupy the same social station, and be friends. Do you still have those little bits of Harold I gave you?"

"Yes. I put them in the pocket of my skirt."

"Save them. I want to paste them back together again."

Laurel stood up. "Now we must go find John Frame," she said. "It's only eight or nine miles. Ten at the most."

12

WHEN THEY GOT TO THE END of the last field before the last woods before the bridge, John was waiting for them. He had seen them a mile off, from the top of his tree. He knelt down in the road and took the hem of Alice's dress and kissed it. "John Frame at your service," he said, and then he looked up at Laurel. "I knew you would put it over them."

Alice reached her hand out to him, like a queen, and he stood up and kissed it. Then he stepped back and put his hands behind his back. He was blushing. He looked at Laurel. "I wish Mr. Regius could have lived to see this. They killed him by sending him out that night. He brought me pork and candles on the way, as you told him to, but his heart gave out before he reached Saltfield."

Laurel crossed herself. "God give him rest. We must have driven past him."

"My stablemaster?" Alice said.

John nodded. "Yes, mistress. Now, with your permission, we should clear off the road. I have a warm, dry place, beneath your least needs and deservings, I know, but safe."

He led them over a low stone fence and into the woods. "Step where I step. No use leaving tracks, is there? See that line of walnut trees? That's our goal. My cave is under the third one, so you can always find it."

When they reached the tree, he stepped up onto a thick root and patted the tree trunk as if it were a favorite horse. Then he looked down. Under the root was a large, flat stone. "You must slide in between the stone and the root. Sit down and lean back and let yourself go. Nothing easier."

The opening looked very small.

"I'll go down first, and light a candle," John said. He jumped over the root, sat down on the stone, and a second later he was gone. It was as if the ground had swallowed him up.

After a minute his hands reached up and grabbed the root, and he pulled himself out. He looked at Laurel. "You must go first. There's a lamp lit now. Sit on the rock, and I can give you a push."

Laurel sat down.

"Good. Now, just lean back a bit. A bit more. And keep your arms down. You don't want to pull them out of your shoulders on your way. Forward a bit more? Perfect."

He put both hands on her shoulders and pushed. She sped through the hole in an instant and hit the floor, hard. She was in a large underground room. A lamp was burning on a low shelf that had been dug out of the wall. There were shadows everywhere.

John poked his head through the entrance. "Are you all right? Want your satchel?"

"Yes. Thank you."

"It's an underground house, nearly, don't you think? Are you ready for the mistress?"

"Yes, I suppose so."

"Excellent." He pulled his head back, and Laurel stood waiting for Alice. Her satchel dropped at her feet. She picked it up and put it aside. She heard them talking, and then John looked in again. "The mistress wants to see my spring. It won't be long."

She heard them walking off. She felt suddenly sad. She decided to explore. She lit two candles from the lamp and looked around. The place was very homey. There was a low table in the middle of the room, two three-legged stools, a short bench, a wide bed with fur blankets, a cabinet, a small iron fireplace with a grate on top for cooking, and a trunk full of books and papers.

She sat on one of the stools and looked at his books. They were all old, and all about building and engineering and farming.

After a while, there were voices outside again, and then John put his head in. "Are you ready?"

"Yes."

Alice's feet and legs poked through. Laurel reached up and held them, guiding her down slowly for a little way, and then kept her from falling when she dropped in. Alice brushed down her skirt and looked around. "What a wonderful servant he is. He knows everything about everything. Don't you think?"

"Yes, mistress."

"I told him about my daffodil. In the glass? I told him our whole adventure. He was dazzled."

He put his head in. "May I come down?"

They stepped back, and he dropped in. He was a little too tall for the cave, so he had to walk with his head bent. "Tea?"

He made tea, and served biscuits and blackberry conserve with it, and by the time they were finished, it was 4:30 by the brass clock next to the stove. "Tomorrow I'll make you a place where you can scrub up properly," he said. "For now there's a washbasin outside next to the first tree. When you're ready, I'll tuck you in."

"Isn't it too early to sleep?" Alice asked.

"Whatever you wish, mistress, but you've had a soldier's day, and it's nearly dark outside. I'll leave you to get ready."

Alice smiled and said she was sure he knew best. When they were side by side in his bed, he came back and covered them with furs. "I'll stand watch. I do that sometimes, just as a drill."

"A drill for what?" Alice asked.

"Guarding you. Now, go to sleep."

"Will you guard us when we go to my funeral?"

"Are you going to do that?"

"Yes."

"I'll guard you wherever you go."

Alice sat up. "It's tomorrow!"

"All the more reason to go to sleep early."

She looked down at Laurel. "What will I wear? I can't go to my funeral dressed like this."

"You must wear something warm," Laurel said. She was feeling very sleepy. "That's first."

Alice smiled at her. "And you must have something beautiful to wear, too."

Laurel got up on her elbow. "It's best if no one notices us."

"Yes yes yes, but we mustn't look common."

"You could never look common, mistress," John said. "You might as well expect the sun to look like a candle."

Alice lay back down. "Still, I'll not go in this dress. I must have something different."

"Sleep, mistress," John said. "I'll see after you."

They slept the whole night without moving, and woke up to the sound of John making tea on the stove. The low table in the middle of the cave was set for breakfast, and in the middle of the table, next to a candle, was Alice's daffodil. Two dresses were hanging from a rope in the ceiling, one mustard-yellow and the other dark green. John spooned some tea into a pot. "I measured you both, with a piece of string, after you'd fallen asleep. Did you sleep well?"

"How did you get them?" Alice asked.

"I nipped up the drainpipe and in through the window. Dark as the inside of a box, so I couldn't tell colors, just length. Yours is the gold one, if I measured properly."

Alice took a deep breath and let it out slowly. "That was the bravest thing anyone could ever do. You mustn't ever do something like that again, unless you tell me first."

"The truth is, mistress, I want to make it up to you, because I let them carry you away that night. It should have been a warning to me, them sending Mr. Regius to town in the dark of night, God rest his soul. I should have stayed up near the road, and tagged a ride with you. You were the one being brave and true to the best, and I was sleeping, there's the truth of it."

Alice looked at Laurel. "He has such a noble heart."

He left the cave, and they got out of bed. "How do you suppose he measured us?" Alice asked. "You don't think he pulled down the covers, do you?"

"I have no idea, mistress."

"It must have been difficult, don't you think? Unless we were lying straight as boards. We must have been."

Laurel and Alice put on their dresses and called to John, and he helped them out and brought them to their washing room, which he had made near the spring, with three blankets and some ropes. He couldn't give them hot water, he said, because that would make clouds of steam, and someone might see it, but he could give them warm water, which would only make a little mist. They washed as best they could, and when they came back to the cave he gave them breakfast—gruel laced with strawberry preserves, and more tea.

"Laurel is no kitchen maid," John said when they were done, "but we'll have to make do. She can take care of the dishes and pot, and I will take you on a bit of a tour of your lands. We have lots of time before you have to be ready."

Alice looked at Laurel. "Ought I?"

"If you wish. You needn't get fancy until noon, so there's a lot of time."

"Well, then, perhaps I should. I don't like to see you doing dishes. We are servants, together, after all."

"If I may suggest, mistress," John said. "It's a steward's duty to place members of the staff where they're needed most. Laurel knows that. And you will never be a servant while I'm alive."

Laurel was beginning to get angry, but she tried not to show it. "I've never been placed anywhere," she said.

"Not only that, but you haven't been in the employ of the Quality before, either."

Laurel turned away and started to pile the dishes and spoons into the pot.

"I have a net for them," John said. "I'll take them outside, and you can wash them in the spring. We'll be gone two hours or more, so you also ought to get in a bit of laundry."

They were gone until noon, and by the time they got back, Laurel had washed Alice's stockings and underwear, so that she would have something fresh for her funeral, and dried them behind the stove, and learned how to get out without hurting herself, by standing on a stool and grabbing a narrow root and twisting and pulling at the same time.

"We've seen ever so much," Alice said. "There's an old bridge downstream from the new one, and we made a big half circle from behind the manor, where the first house was, and then around to the chapel. They're digging a grave. With picks. It must be ever so hard work. I wonder what they put in my coffin. John thinks a few bags of sand, and so do I."

They had a little bread, and then they took their dresses and went out to the dressing room that John had made and put them on.

Laurel had never owned a dress that went on over her head, or one that was made out of silk. Her dresses had all been wool, and they had all buttoned up the front, and they had all been a little bit scratchy. She took the dress down from the rope. The cold, slippery silk made her shiver.

She took a deep breath, lifted the dress over her head, and began working her way through it. It was pitch dark in there, and the silk clung to her arms and face. She began to get dizzy. She got her right elbow up past the waist and felt around for the armhole. When she found it, she stopped for a moment and tried to pull the material away from her face so that she could breathe but she couldn't.

She straightened out her left arm and got it through the left sleeve and pulled the right sleeve down until her right hand was free, and then she pushed all the material down past her face until her nose was out. Then she just stood there, panting, as if she had been reborn. Alice was standing behind her. "Put your arms up straight again, and I'll pull it down the rest of the way. Stand quite still. Good. I'll button your back."

Laurel stood still, and Alice buttoned her up. There were a lot of very small buttons, and Alice's hands were cold and stiff, so it took a long time. The soft, heavy silk across her shoulders and the rich green of the long, narrow sleeves made her feel like a woman.

"There. Now stay still. I'm going to comb out your beautiful red hair. We'll need a bonnet to put it under, or a black cloth, or something. And mourner's bands. Or a sash? What do you think?"

"We're bound to attract attention the way we are," Laurel said.

"Green is the perfect color for your hair," Alice said. "John will get us something to cover ourselves up. I don't want quarreling when I marry. I've been thinking about it. It's almost better not to marry at all than it is to quarrel all the time. A young lady alone in the world must find someone she's not likely to quarrel with."

She came around and stood in front of Laurel and held her arms. "Isn't that the first consideration? More important than position or social station? Or riches?"

"Likely so," Laurel said.

Alice took hold of Laurel's hands and stepped back. "I wish John had brought shoes. I can see him in my mind's eye climbing down the wall with my daffodil in his hand and these dresses over his shoulder. It makes my whole frame quiver."

Laurel put her foot out. The silk hem was a little short, touching her ankle. "We'll take small steps, and when we stand, no one will be able to see what sort of shoes we have."

Alice squeezed Laurel's hands. "Have you ever been to a ball?"

"No, not ever. I've been to weddings where there was dancing, but they were country weddings, and I was just watching."

"I never was at one, either. I went to dancing classes when I was very tiny. There were boys, of course, and we all wore gloves. Would you like to see what we learned? We never did more than the simplest, simplest things, most often in line, but sometimes in pairs. You just count. One two three, one two three, one two three."

Laurel watched her stepping to the side, and back, and forward, and started to copy her, and they danced slowly around their dressing room, stepping carefully over roots, and when they had gone twice around, they stopped and curtsied to each other.

"It was kind of you to give me this dance, Miss Bybank," Alice said.

Laurel spread her hands. "Not at all. My pleasure, Miss Plunderell."

"Oh, a privilege, dear Laurel."

"Likewise on my side, dear Alice."

John tapped on one of the blankets. "Mistress Alice? Laurel? Are you anywhere near ready?"

They stood looking at each other.

"You called me by my name," Alice said.

"Yes," Laurel said.

"Don't stop, now that we're friends."

13

JOHN HAD THREE COATS. The first was a shepherd's coat, with the fur turned inside, that he wore when he was going to be sitting outside all night. The second was an old opera cloak that he used as a tablecloth. The third was a heavy coachman's coat which had belonged to Mr. Regius's younger brother.

To go to the funeral, John wore the shepherd's coat, Laurel wore the opera cloak with the hood over her hair, and Alice wore the coachman's coat. She had sneezed a few times before they left, so John and Laurel insisted that she button it up to the neck, at least until she got inside the chapel. She also wore a black kerchief that Laurel had cut out of the lining of her coat and folded and pinned to look like a bonnet.

They walked through the woods in the direction of the chapel for a long distance, and then waited near the road for the household to go by. First in line was a hearse with enormous wheels and glass sides. Alice's coffin, with bright brass handles, rode inside on a bed of black velvet. Behind the hearse came a coach, very high, pulled by four horses with fountains of black feathers coming out of their necks. The curtains on the back windows were drawn, to protect the grieving aunt and uncle from the eyes of ordinary people, but the front ones were open and Laurel and Alice and John could see the Reverend Father Grote-Pinckney sitting up very straight and holding a high hat against his chest.

Behind the coach, on foot, came Mr. Lloyd in a black suit and black gloves and a hat trimmed with black ribbon. Behind him came the cook, her assistant, and Helen.

Laurel touched John's arm. "Do you see the girl? Lord Stayne booted her out. I saw it."

They waited for a minute after the procession was out of sight, and then went out onto the road and followed. As they walked along, Alice told John about the fight between her aunt and uncle. "I know it's not the least bit funny, seeing a lady's wig flying through the air. Isn't that true, Laurel? Fat little bald ladies shouldn't be laughed at? Of course, I didn't laugh when it was coming to pass directly under my eyes."

"What did you do, mistress?" John asked.

Alice looked at Laurel, and then back at John. "A lady had best not say," she said. "But there she was, with the little line of black fuzz on top of her head blowing in the breeze, and my uncle hippity-hoppitying across the snow and picking up her hair and hippity-hoppitying back." She started to giggle, and every once in a while as they went along she would put her hand over her mouth and giggle again.

They came in sight of the chapel, and stopped.

Alice touched Laurel's arm. "There's my grave. In the back corner of the churchyard? Do you see it?"

"Yes. It's in a very pretty spot."

"Perhaps I should hang back, mistress," John said. "I'm not a regular attender at church, and I don't mind the cold."

"You don't want to come?"

John looked up to the sky. "I prefer not to pray for you as if you were dead, or even to pretend to, but whatever you want me to do is right."

"You would be sad if I died?"

"Please don't say things like that, mistress. You know I would."

The church bell began to ring. The clapper had been wrapped in cloth, so it sounded like a drum. They were silent until it stopped.

"You must come as far as the path to the chapel, John, and wait," Alice said. "Is that best, do you think?"

"Whatever you want is best."

"Good. We should hurry."

When Laurel and Alice reached the chapel porch, the faithful were already singing the first verse of "For All the Saints." The chapel was jammed, and it seemed that they wouldn't be able to get inside, but then Alice opened her coat to show her dress, and an old man standing at the door started pushing people aside to make way for them. "Step aside for the lady," he said, and they squeezed through the door and got in among the people standing against the back wall.

When the congregation had sung *Amen*, and the opening prayers had been said, and everyone with a seat was kneeling, Alice stood out like a flower against a dark hedge. If Lord and Lady Stayne, who were in the front row, had turned around they would instantly have recognized her. But they kept their eyes on the Reverend Grote-Pinckney, and the Reverend Grote-Pinckney kept moving his eyes back and forth between them and his prayer book, every once in a while looking at the painting of the young woman in the ruined garden, which had been put on an easel next to the coffin.

There were many prayers and many passages from the Bible, and after a while Alice leaned over and whispered in Laurel's ear, "It's not what I thought. Are your feet cold?"

Laurel nodded her head. "A little."

"Everyone looks sad, but no one seems to be grieving."

"I'm sure they feel your loss very deeply."

"Yes, I suppose so. Still, it's not what I expected." She started to cough, and the man who had cleared the way for them came over with a little cane chair and made her sit. After a minute she stopped and looked up to show that she was all right.

Father Grote-Pinckney climbed up into the pulpit, looked out over his audience, cleared his throat and began to speak. He spoke, first, of the *heavenly regions where all is bliss,* the *sacred valleys amid the clouds, where God's blessed live in peace eternal,* and the *High Home of Splendor*. After ten or fifteen minutes of such word pictures, he spoke of *Our Dear Departed Angel* and *Our Absent Sweet Companion on the Way*, who was *Free from the Burden of this Sinful Flesh, this House of Clay*. Finally, he made much of the fact that *Her Golden Hair Has Now Become Her Golden Crown*. Then, suddenly, he said *Amen* and left the pulpit.

Laurel reached down and felt Alice's forehead, to see if she had a fever. It seemed perfectly cool.

Nearby, a very old lady, standing stiff and still, started to cry. Laurel had seen strangers cry at funerals before, men and women who were grieving not for the person in the coffin but for their own dead children and parents and brothers and sisters and friends. Looking at the old lady, she remembered Father Simpson and Granny Piersall and St. Anne's Church, and she began to cry, too. Alice tugged on her skirt, and she looked away and made herself stop.

The Reverend Father Grote-Pinckney made a circle around the coffin, blessing it, and then six big men in stiff collars picked it up and followed him slowly down the narrow aisle. Each man held on with both hands, and slid down the aisle sideways. Lord and Lady Stayne came behind them, looking down at the floor. He was wearing his long black coat, with a wide loop of black ribbon around his left sleeve, and she had a droopy black hat with a black velvet bow. She had hold of his arm and was leaning her whole weight on it, as if she didn't have the strength to walk by herself.

Laurel decided that she wanted them to know right now, right in the middle of God's Church, that the ghost of one of their victims was back to haunt them. She turned toward the aisle and moved forward half a step so that she was shielding Alice from view, and pushed back her hood and waited for them to pass.

The coffin went slowly by, with the men making little grunts and groans, and then came Lord and Lady Stayne, still looking down at the floor. Laurel's heart was pounding, but she was determined that they would not pass by without seeing her. She moved her shoulders, and Lord Stayne looked up at her. His eyes opened wide and his mouth dropped. She stuck her tongue out at him, and he looked away, and a few seconds later he was out the door.

She reached down and took Alice by the hand. "I let him see me. Come along. Hurry."

Alice put her hand to her mouth. "Truly?"

"Don't worry. He's out the door. Come."

Alice didn't move. Her face was pale, almost gray.

"Alice? Please?"

Laurel pulled her out of her chair and through the crowd to the right side of the chapel, down the aisle and out through a side door into the open. The procession was going around the other side of the chapel, toward the churchyard, so they were suddenly alone.

"He saw you?"

"I let him. I'm not sorry. No one should be allowed to mock God this way and not have a day of reckoning."

Alice looked at her. "You must be the bravest female in England."

"And also proud and vain, but it's done. He doesn't know you're anywhere near. He thinks you're far away up in heaven, so you're safe. Are you well? Do you want to rest?"

"I never want to go to a funeral of mine again. Dying isn't a bit worth it. What do we do now?"

Laurel stepped away from the wall and looked toward the road where John was standing. He waved and pointed toward the woods, and she and Alice hurried in that direction, always keeping the chapel between them and Alice's grave. When they were safely among the trees, they stopped and waited for him. Alice's nose was running. "As soon as we get back to John's, you must go to bed. We'll tuck you in with some hot tea and honey."

"You're a hero," Alice said. "Where's John?"

"He's coming. You'll go to bed as soon as we get back?"

"If you say so. I wish he had seen me, too. Do you think they worry about us in heaven? The people who are already there, like my papa and mama?"

"No, I don't think so. I've thought a lot about it. They remember us, and they pray for us, but prayer is like play for them. All mothers in heaven pray for their children, and if the children die first, they pray for their mothers and fathers. Do you know St. Augustine? His mother was the most famous praying mother of all, except for Mary the Mother of Our Lord. St. Monica."

John came, and they hurried back to his cave. After Alice had been tucked tightly in bed, she asked Laurel to tell her the story of St. Monica, as long as there weren't any dead children in it.

Laurel shook her head. "No dead children. It all happened a thousand years ago, before England was even a country. There was a man, and his name was Augustine, and he was very very clever and quick. And he had a good heart under it all. All the university masters of his time were afraid of him because he was able to make the silliest idea sound truer than the truth. He went to a certain school, not a Christian school, and in no time he became a master himself, and everybody flocked to him. And he wrote books, of course, and went here and there and everywhere making speeches, and gathering disciples, and living a riotous life in unsavory lodgings. All of this put his eternal soul in danger, of course. He was always suspended over the Pit, and the wide and pleasant roads of lust and vanity seemed to stretch forever in front of him. He knew in his heart he was a great sinner, and he was very restless and unhappy, but he kept on.

"Now Augustine had a mother, Monica, and all the while he was giving himself to riotous living, she was praying for him, that he would give up his dazzling worldly ideas and turn to the Truth. She prayed night and day, in season and out, that God would set his life aright. And she never gave up hope. She was sure that God was hearing her prayers. And after a long time He sent the Holy Ghost down to Augustine and changed his heart. He became a Christian, and many of his followers, too, and in no time at all he was a great leader in the Church, and a bishop.

"Well, during these days his mother grew sick and died, but she knew that no victory in this world is free from danger, so even after she was in heaven she continued to beseech God to keep him in the right way, now that he had found it. Nobody knew she was praying, of course, except Augustine, and when they sent him to be the Bishop of Africa, he had a vision of her standing on the dock as his ship left, with her hands folded in prayer. And when he died and went to heaven, she was the first one to meet him, and they're both still there, and they see each other every day. Isn't that lovely?"

Alice didn't answer. She was fast asleep.

14

LAUREL SLEPT ON THE FLOOR, with some furs under her and the opera cloak on top, and John slept on a chair, with his feet on the table. Sometime in the middle of the night Laurel sat up, eyes wide open. She knew where the treasure was. It was under the dock, where August's mother had bid her son goodbye.

"John?" she whispered.

He didn't answer.

She sat in the silent darkness, thinking. Could someone else have solved the riddle and gotten the treasure and carried it away? Not likely. Not many people remembered St. Augustine, especially among the Protestants. She pushed back the cloak. She wanted to get up and climb out of the cave and get down to the river while it was still dark, walk across, find the box in the first light of day and bring it back and leave it right outside the entrance, where John would find it when he went out. But she didn't dare. She lay back down again, and pulled up the cloak, and shut her eyes. She was sure she would never get back to sleep.

When she woke up, John's chair was empty. She sat up. Had she told him about the treasure during the night and forgotten about it? No. If she had told him, they would have been up talking all night, making plans. She turned to the bed. Alice was sitting up reading a book.

"I know where the treasure is," she said. "It's under the dock. August's mother is St. Monica. It's simple as simple, when you think about it."

Alice looked up. "Look what John did. He got me my book of maps. Isn't he absolutely the most marvelous person ever?"

"The riddle isn't about August," Laurel said. "It's about Augustine."

"Yes. We must ask John about it. He'll know what we ought to do."

"Where is he?"

"Prowling about. He'll be coming back directly. His judgment will be best."

There was boiling water on the grate, and Laurel started to make a pot of tea. While it was steeping, she climbed out of the cave and went to the spring and washed her hands and face. Even the water coming up out of the ground was cold as ice. The only sound was the water splashing on a rock. After a while she walked to the edge of the woods and looked across the river at the dock. She had the right to get the treasure. She had solved the riddle, and solvers should be allowed to be finders. Besides, she could wiggle into smaller spaces than John, and he ought to be looking after Alice, anyway. And now was the time, today or tonight. What if the Reverend Grote-Pinckney, during his after-funeral visit at the manor, should happen to bring up the story of St. Augustine, which he might if the talk turned to Africa or the Early Church, and they guessed?

The sooner the treasure was fetched, the better. There were gray places on the river, but the ice looked solid enough.

When she got back to the cave, Alice was still alone. She sat down on the bed. "Alice? May I be the one to fetch the treasure? There's no telling how heavy it will be, but I can get into narrower places, and if it's too heavy to carry I can slide it across the river after dark and John can help me carry it back here."

Alice smiled.

"I may?"

"John will know best. Laurel? Do you think, if someone chooses to marry someone of a lower social class, and the higher-class someone is a woman, and the man would never ask her on his own, it would be acceptable if she sent a friend to him to tell him how she felt?"

"Do you want me to do that with John?"

"I don't know. He's won my heart and soul forever." She leaned forward and took Laurel's hand. "Are we rivals? I bind you to tell me the truth about that."

"Alice, I'm fourteen."

"That doesn't signify, ever. Have I broken your heart?"

Laurel shook her head. "No, but I'm afraid for you, if the truth be told, because it's so sudden. In the woods when he stepped onto the road in front of me, the day I came to the manor? He was very pleasant to me. Well, gallant. He was very gallant. We belong in the same service and the same class, and anyone with half an eye can see that he's the most faithful person in the world, but I wouldn't be pledged to anyone now, no matter who."

Alice leaned back again. "You're wise beyond your years. He's handsome, too, don't you think? He has the hands of an angel. You must love him. Everyone in the world must."

Laurel got off the bed and went to the teapot. "He's very handsome, and I did think of him as a husband, but only the way little girls do, in a storybook way."

"You were never a little girl."

"Yes, I was, just not anymore. Meeting murderers pushes you along."

"Were you hoping to save him for later?"

"No."

"I've made you sad, though, I know I have, taking him away from you."

Laurel poured some tea for Alice and put sugar in it and brought it to her and sat back down. "You're my friend now, and I never had one before. That's a great step for me. I don't need to find a husband. Truly I don't."

Alice smiled at her. "Good. And we are friends, forever and ever. Wasn't it fine, dancing in the woods yesterday? I'll never forget it. Will you?"

"Never. John wrote a poem about you. Did he tell you that? I saw it in his steward's book. About him standing under your window. I believe he wanted me to see it, so I would know he had already given his heart away."

Alice shifted around in bed, almost spilling her tea. "So, he loved me even when he thought it was hopeless. Was ever a maiden so blessed?"

They heard John outside. "May I come in?"

Alice put her finger to her lips. "You'll talk to him? You'll know best what to say."

Laurel nodded. "As soon as it seems right."

John came in, and Laurel immediately told him where the treasure was. "You must get me an iron bar, in case it needs prying loose," she said. "I'll go at the last light, when the river is in deep shadow, and as soon as I get it loose, I'll slide it back. Of course, it could be quite small, small enough to carry."

John looked at Alice. "I should be the one to get it."

"You can watch me from the woods," Laurel said. "I'm tall, but I fit into smaller spaces, and I know how to use a bar. Do you have one?"

"That's not girls' work."

Laurel looked at Alice. "The mistress thought I could, and you'll be closer to her to watch over her. And if I can't get it free, you can come over after dark and help me. I'll go at sunset."

"You know best, John," Alice said, "and we'll be ruled by you, but Laurel did answer the riddle when nobody else could, which makes her very deserving."

He looked at Laurel, and then back at Alice. "She did, but I can't say it's a good idea. He's seen her, so he's bound to be looking out for her. But whatever you wish, mistress."

Laurel smiled. "Thank you, John. And you don't have to worry. He thinks I'm a ghost."

"Just don't come back trying to carry it by yourself. Wait until I come across and fetch you."

At twilight, John and Laurel were standing on the shore looking across at the dock. The water running under the ice was very loud, and Laurel thought she could see big bubbles sliding and skipping along, but that might have been nothing but the light.

"It's black under there," she said.

"Where?"

"The dock, but my eyes will get used to it."

"Go in a straight line from here and you'll be safe as home in bed. There's something of a swirl there, to the left, that might be chewing away at the ice, but a straight road from here, you're safe. You know how to use the bar. Sorry it's so heavy. You still have Mistress Alice's good dress on under my coat."

"Pardon?"

"Mistress Alice's green dress. You still have it on."

"Yes. I'll need it to keep me warm. She told me to wear it."

She stepped out onto the river, fixed her eyes on the end of the dock, and walked toward it, pretending that the ice was solid ground. In half a minute she was standing under the end of the dock, looking up. The stone pilings were connected by a line of iron rods with oak planks bolted to them. The ice underneath her feet was rough, and there were tree branches sticking up through it.

She shifted the bar to her left hand and began working her way slowly toward the shore, stopping at each piling and examining it in the fading light. When she got to the edge of the ice, where the shore began to slope up, she had to duck her head. She was sure she knew where the treasure was, if it hadn't already been found and taken away. It was tucked into the tight three-sided space between the last piling, the riverbank, and the floor of the dock.

Her skirt caught on something and ripped. She pulled it loose, crawled forward, reached around behind the last pillar on the right, and put her hand on the treasure chest. It was about the size of a toolbox, and it was bolted to a plank which had become rotten from the damp ground. There was a clasp on the front, but she couldn't tell whether it was locked or not.

She rolled onto her back, moved the bar to her right hand, and pushed the narrow end of it between the chest and the floor. The chest immediately came loose and broke open. Diamonds, rubies, strings of pearls, gold coins, rings, earrings, brooches, and bracelets came flooding down on her like coal out of a scuttle. They rolled and bounced and skittered left and right, making an awful noise. When it was over, she slid forward and looked around.

She couldn't believe that so much had come out of a box only about a foot and a half long and eight inches high. There seemed to be more and more everywhere she looked.

When everything under the dock had been put back in the box, she sat down. Her hands were shaking. She hugged herself to get them warm, and then dashed out onto the river, slipped and fell, made a quick circle, throwing everything she picked up into her skirt and leaving little bloody marks on the ice.

When she was back underneath, she sat down and packed the jewels and coins and bracelets as neatly as she could and closed the lid, bending the clasp so it wouldn't come open again. Looking far out, she saw a few jewels still in the open. The diamonds were getting lost in the ice, but the rubies and emeralds seemed to get brighter as it got darker. She said a prayer, and waited for John.

She heard a crunching sound. Someone was coming down the road toward the dock. She backed as quietly as she could into the narrowest space next to the shortest piling and waited.

The man was carrying a lantern. Maybe somebody came down to this dock every night for some reason. Maybe somebody was coming to fish through the ice. People did that all the time. Yes, that was probably it. She prayed that he would walk downriver, or upriver, before he cut his hole. He walked out onto the dock and stopped about halfway. Then he turned and walked back and came down the bank, slipping and sliding.

Suddenly she was looking into the light.

"Sewer rat," Lord Stayne said. He took out a knife. "Do you know what servants who abandon their mistresses and let them die deserve? Drawing and quartering, dear child, slowly. Catholics are the most brazen people in the world. Primitive. You pry the secret from our poor dear niece, lie to us about it, steal her dress, go to her funeral. God will damn you to eternal fire. And the worst crime is trying to steal my inheritance, what I froze in this bloody tomb of a house to get. I am going to cut your heart out of your body right now."

"Alice isn't dead," Laurel said. "She's sick."

"You're lying."

"No, I'm not."

"Swear it on the cross."

"I swear it on the cross."

"And on Satan's pitchfork."

"No. That's a sin."

"Where is she?"

"She's in a cave. She has a cold. I could take you to her, but not in the dark, not even with a lantern, so you can't kill me until daylight."

"Is she dying?"

"All flesh is grass, my Lord."

"Don't give me that priest's answer. Is she dying?"

"Who could say? I can tell you she's coughing more than she ought."

"Then we will keep you until morning."

Laurel didn't move.

"We'll bring her flowers, ha-ha-ha. Truly. Would I lie to you at a time like this? Do you see this knife? If you don't come out of there, I will come and stick it in your chest. You can believe that. I saw you running about on the ice quite by accident, showing that God, after all, favors his favorite children. You see how everything comes out right for those who do their best and are willing to sacrifice to accomplish great things? That's a good lesson for you to ponder."

"If a girl does her work, and trusts God," Laurel said, "nobody in the world can harm her soul."

"Are you mocking me?"

"No, my Lord."

"Climb out."

"Yes, my Lord."

"Don't be sly, don't be sly. Bring the chest along with you. Leave the bar just there. That's the girl."

She came out, bumping her head, and stood in front of him. "You are a cruel man, sir," she said, her voice shaking, "but you are still among the living, and have time to repent and obtain God's mercy."

He leaned into her face. "I will do a jig on your grave," he said. His breath smelled of brandy. "You have the chest, but I have the knife. Now, attention, walk along beside me. Good scheme? None better. I'll gag you and lock you in the garden house until everyone is asleep, and then we'll climb up to Lady Stayne's room and lay the treasure at her feet. Then she'll know if she's dealing with a fool or not."

They went up the bank and started along the road toward the house. Laurel glanced at the knife. It was very long, and pointed at the end. He smiled and wiggled his eyebrows. "I must tell you, the Pope in Rome is a friend of mine, and if you try to run away I will kill you and then I will go and tell him how evil you were, and he will make God lock your soul up in hell, where it will burn for all eternity."

Laurel started walking a little bit faster. "The Pope wouldn't do that. If I must die, I will not allow His Holiness to be slandered. Catholics are not as stupid as you think."

"Don't walk so fast."

She slowed down, still looking left and right for a place to escape. She saw a patch of ice ahead. That would be where she would fly, as soon as he got his feet on it. He started to shift to the left, so that he wouldn't step on it, and as soon as he did, Laurel stopped, turned, took two long steps, jumped over the ditch into the field, and started to run, aiming for the woods to the left of the house. Her skirt slowed her down, and she couldn't hitch it up because she was carrying the treasure chest, but she was determined not to let it go unless he was right on top of her. The knife flew past her and twisted into the snow, bouncing once. The squeak of the lantern handle seemed very close, and she was about to drop the chest when there was the sound of glass breaking, and he cursed.

She ran faster.

She kept running until she was into the first trees and out of the moonlight, and then she stopped. Lord Stayne was coming, but he was on a path that cut halfway between her and the house, as if he couldn't make up his mind which way to go.

She went deeper into the woods, weaving in and out and trying to keep parallel with the river. She tripped and fell, and got caught in some branches as she was getting up, but she didn't stop.

After a while she stopped again and listened, and then she started downhill. After a minute the woods thinned out and she could see the foggy river below. She was about three hundred yards downriver, but she could see the bridge clearly. She hated the idea of crossing the ice again, in a place John didn't know, but she was determined not to stop until she was on the other side.

She looked toward the bridge again. John was running across it toward the manor. She stood up and waved, but he kept running. "Damn!" she said. "Excuse me, God." She started running toward him, waving her free arm. He was already across the bridge and partway up the road when he stopped. Two men were coming down toward him with lanterns. He looked her way, turned, and started in the opposite direction. She crouched down until they were out of sight, and then ran to the bridge and crossed it and went in among the trees and waited. She had been sweating, and now she started shivering. The line of walnut trees marking John's cave stood out clearly in the moonlight. She waited for him but he didn't come, so she finally went to the cave and dropped inside.

"Alice?"

There was no answer.

She blew up the fire and lit a candle. "I know she's all right," she whispered. "John saw after her. He has some other hiding place. That's why he didn't come and try to rescue me right away."

She made some tea. She prayed. She worried. She wanted to take off her silk dress, which was wet and filthy, and put on her old brown one, but she couldn't without someone to help with the buttons. She sat down and looked into the fire. "I must just be patient and wait."

After a while there was a noise outside, and John dropped in. He looked at the treasure on the floor, and then at her. "You're a wonder. An absolute wonder. You know that, don't you?"

"That's not for me to say. Where's Alice?"

"I put her on the road to Saltfield, to get help, in case they caught us both. You and I, I mean. I came back here, and after a bit she and I went down to the river to watch, but just as I was about to come across, there all of a sudden was Lord S. taking you out from under the dock. As soon as she was safely on her way, I came after you. How did you get away from him?"

"I ran. We should go after her."

"I ought."

"No. I must go, too."

"You've already done too much. You'll be safer here. I'll bring her. We shan't go anywhere else, I promise."

Laurel shook her head. "No."

They blew out the candle, left the treasure chest where it was, climbed out, and started toward town. After a few minutes, Laurel got an idea. "I've a clean shroud in my satchel. What if we were to dress Alice in it, and put some flour on her face. Have you any white flour?"

"A little."

"That's all we need. I'll put some on Alice's face and hands, get a candle for her to hold, stand her a nice safe distance from the entrance, but still close enough for them to see her, hide and howl? They open the front door, and there in front of them is the ghost of Alice Plunderell, the shroud tied tight around her face, moaning, if she can do it. Of course, we won't do any of it unless she wants it. I think it will drive them simply out of their minds. Anybody who knows as little about Catholics as they do certainly has no spiritual training at all and will believe anything."

"But only if she wants to."

"Naturally, only if she wants to."

They heard a horse coming along the road, and moved to the side. It came around the bend going faster than any horse should go at night, even in bright moonlight. Harold Pomfret-Watkin was in front, with Alice sitting behind him. Laurel called out to them, and they stopped. Alice slid off the horse backward, almost falling down, and ran to Laurel and embraced her. "Laurel, oh, Laurel, thank God they didn't kill you."

"Well," Harold Pomfret-Watkin said. "Well well well, this is splendid, I must say."

Alice and Laurel let go of each other.

Harold Pomfret-Watkin hit his boot with his riding crop. "Absolutely splendid, don't you agree?" He looked at John. "Who are you?"

"John Frame. I'm steward of Plunderell Manor, or will be when we win our way back. And there's a scheme for that. Shall I tell it to you?"

"Excellent, certainly, but first I must speak a word to Laurel, if I may make bold to call her by her Christian name. May I, dear Laurel?"

"If you wish, sir." She turned to Alice. "You saw I found the treasure?"

Alice embraced her again. "You're a miracle. The biggest diamond is yours."

Harold Pomfret-Watkin coughed. "May I break in? I have a speech to deliver. Laurel Bybank, there you stand in the moonlight in your tattered dress, a perfect example of the good old feudal spirit still alive in this modern world. I am an exceedingly democratic person myself, as you will soon discover, but I must say your loyalty to your mistress warms my heart." He turned to Alice. "Did you know she wrote me a postal card? Took me to task for not knowing my chapters and verses in the Gospel. That was the trigger. I had to come see her and find out if everything else she had said was true. I'm baring my soul here. Let's have an end to it. Will you forgive me or not, that I did not see your honest soul at once?"

"Yes, I will," Laurel said. "Not that you need apologize."

"Spoken like a lady. Now, what's your scheme?"

John told him of the idea of making Alice look like a ghost, and he shook his head. "Clearly your brains are growing tired. These are two grownup people. They won't be fooled." He held his finger in the air. "But at the moment they're completely off-balance and a bit brain-tired themselves. A child could send them off simply by telling them to go, and that's what we'll do. We'll walk into the house and tell them to be gone, their tenure is up, lease expired. It's your home, yes? You're of age. And the treasure is yours now, isn't it?" He looked at Laurel. "There were things of value in that box you found, weren't there?"

"Oh, yes. Jewels and jewels."

"Quite. Well, then, Alice Punderell, you have them just where you need them to be. Did I ever tell you what my mother used to say to me? She used to sit me on her lap and say, 'Harry, dear, all anyone needs in this world is a good cause, and money, and powerful friends.' Well, now that I'm here, you have them all. And what do they have? A third-rate domestic staff. We must go and face them down this instant, when they're tired and fogged, and, thanks to my sudden arrival, we're fresh as daisies. Agreed?"

Everyone agreed, so Harold Pomfret-Watkin put Laurel and Alice up on his horse and they went as fast as they could to the manor. When they arrived, all four went to the door and knocked loudly. Mr. Lloyd opened it, and Harold Pomfret-Watkin pushed his way inside. "Tell me, my man, who are you?" he asked.

Mr. Lloyd was staring at Laurel. She put back her hood, smiled, and curtsied to him. He looked at Harold Pomfret-Watkin. "I'm the steward here," he said.

Harold Pomfret-Watkin put up one finger. "Alas for you, little man, that is no longer the case. A misfortune for you, but not, happily, for the stewards' profession. This fine gentleman to my left, Mr. John Frame, is steward here. You will henceforward do what he directs. To his left is Mistress Alice Plunderell, who owns this noble pile, and the plucky and ravishing creature to her left is Miss Laurel Bybank, whom you know slightly. I am their lifelong friend, Harold Pomfret-Watkin. You perhaps know the name. Mines? Steamships? Did you tell me your Christian name?"

"Albert, sir."

"Excellent. Well, Albert, I must tell you that the days of Lord and Lady Stayne in this house are over."

Lord Stayne came down the stairs. He was in his silk dressing gown and black boots. "Here, here, what is this? What are you doing, coming into a household of grief this way?"

Harold Pomfret-Watkin began clapping his hands. "Excellent, dear Stayne, but not excellent enough. You are done in this house, and I'm here to tell you the sooner you're out, the better."

Lord Stayne pointed at Laurel. "This girl, innocent as she looks, is a classless Irish Catholic murderer and a swindler. She has taken you in, sir."

Harold Pomfret-Watkin took a step toward him. "I warn you sir, you are speaking of the woman I love. Were these not modern times, I would challenge you to a duel." He looked up the stairs. Lady Stayne had started down, and was on the landing. "Ah, Lady Stayne? Permit me to introduce myself. Harold Pomfret-Watkin. Pomfret Shipping? Watkin's soap? I am here to announce your eviction. The constable will be coming to collect you in the morning, but we are willing to allow you to leave freely tonight, for the sake of being rid of the clutter."

She took a deep breath. "I have never been so insulted in my life."

Harold Pomfret-Watkin shook his head. "I am losing some of my good humor, madame. Be advised by me. Dab a little extra paste on your wig and get out there into the windy world. Alice Plunderell is going to sleep here tonight, and she doesn't want you mucking up her property. The jig is entirely finished, I assure you." He looked at Mr. Lloyd. "Albert? The cook is awake, unless she's died or gone deaf. Get her working on a little light refreshment. Tea. Cocoa. Cold meat pie if she has it. Some toast. I'll leave the rest to her. And get a fire in the dining room and set the table. Do you understand?"

Mr. Lloyd bowed slightly. "Yes, sir."

Harold Pomfret-Watkin looked at Lord Stayne. "Still here? Does that mean deafness is catching? We're letting you go, Stayne, only because you're such a bungler at crime, but the magistrates will not take that view, and what they do to you won't be a bit pretty. Do you know my Uncle Caspar Baines? Mother's brother. He's been on the bench for a dozen years or more. Hangs a man or two every week, just to keep himself fit for really serious cases." He looked at John. "Shall we offer them a carriage?"

"As a mercy. They may take it and leave it at the station. I'll hitch up the horses."

Lord Stayne opened his mouth, but nothing came out.

"Wise man," Harold Pomfret-Watkin said. "We're going into the dining room now, and we won't even peek to see what you're doing, but by the end of our midnight supper, you will both be gone."

15

LAUREL OPENED HER EYES and looked around. The room was full of bright sunlight. From the yard came the sound of someone hanging a harness against a wall. She sat up and slid toward the end of her mattress. The straw creaked under her. She was wearing one of Alice's silk nightdresses, pale green with tiny flowers embroidered across the front and down the sleeves. She lifted her right arm and put her nose into the silk. It smelled of lavender.

She was at the foot of Alice's bed. She could see Alice's braid hanging over the lace edge of her pillow. She pulled the blanket around herself and looked at the wall and thought about everything that had happened last night, coming upon Alice and Harold Pomfret-Watkin on the dark road through the woods, telling them her idea for frightening Lord and Lady Stayne, listening while Harold Pomfret-Watkin said it was a silly idea, getting up on his horse behind Alice, knocking on the manor door, standing in the entrance hall while he ordered Lord and Lady Stayne off the property, and then going to bed right after supper because Alice was so tired and had been sick.

She could still see Harold Pomfret-Watkin standing like a soldier, pointing to the door with his stumpy little finger and telling them to leave the house forthwith. They were more than twice his age, but still they had gone. It was amazing. Did rich boys learn to give orders like that at public school? Did their teachers line them up on the playing field every afternoon, summer and winter, and have them put their arms out and point their fingers toward the village? And at night before they went to bed, did the boys have to practice giving orders to each other, saying "Begone!" and "Away!" and "Out with you!" over and over again until they had just the right sneer in their voices, not too much, not too little? Probably. Nobody could be born knowing how to do that.

She pushed back the blankets and got up, crossed the room, and went behind the screen and put on her clean shift and her brown dress. Then, carrying her shoes and her cloak, she went to the bed and looked down at Alice. The blanket was up around her ears. She was breathing softly and smiling.

Laurel left the room, closing the door quietly, went down the old wooden stairs, put on her shoes, and buttoned them as fast as she could. Her plan was to go to the kitchen and start scrubbing it. She could still remember the gritty, greasy feel of the wall under her fingers, and she was sure the dead mouse was waiting for her in the biscuit tin in the cupboard.

As she walked down the dim hall, she heard John's voice. She turned the corner, went past the little room where Mr. Regius had given her soup the first day, and stopped at the kitchen door. John was standing by the sink talking to a woman who was stirring porridge on the stove. He stopped talking and looked at her.

"Please," Laurel said, "I don't mean to intrude."

John shook his head. "Nothing of the sort. We were just speaking about how to bring order to the kitchen. This is Mrs. Hemmings."

Laurel made a slight curtsy. "I'm Laurel Bybank," she said. "I'm very pleased to make your acquaintance. I'd be happy to help put the house back on its feet. I could do some scrubbing?" She looked down at her dress. "All I need is an apron. Or I could do the laundry?"

John came across the kitchen and went past her out the door. "May I speak with you, Laurel?"

He walked quickly down the hall, and she followed him through the dining room, across the entrance hall, and into the trophy room, where there was a fire in the fireplace. He went over to it and stood there. "You're well?" he said.

"Yes. And you?"

"Excellent. I spent the night in my cave. Guarding the treasure."

"That was very wise."

"Yes."

Laurel stood looking at him, waiting for him to say something else, and when he didn't, she looked up at the lion's head on the chimney. "One day, I suppose we'll want to hoist all of these animals out of here. Not first thing, but after a time?"

John frowned at her. "Why?"

"They're Lord Stayne's."

"No, they're not."

"Oh."

"Did he tell you that? Not a bit of it. Been here forever. Liars must lie, as they say. Of course, if Lady Alice chooses to give them the heave, we can be rid of them in an hour. Everyone's going to treat you differently from now on, you know."

"I'm just the same as I ever was."

He shook his head. "Not so. Now you own a diamond. But it's not just the diamond. Least thing. You could take it and throw it in the hole in the river and it wouldn't make a particle of difference. You can't be a servant anymore, and that's flat."

"I'm not sure I know how to be idle. Every house I've lived in, I've always helped to keep."

"John looked down into the fire. "No more."

"I'd not expect pay."

"No matter. I can't let you work for wages, and I can't let you work for no wages. Either way, you take work from someone who needs it. If you don't understand, I don't know how otherwise to say it. Are you sorry you're rich?"

"No."

"I'm glad to hear that. Hating money is an offense to the poor, as Mr. Regius used to say. Please don't be angry with me. I'm not scolding you."

Laurel shook her head. "I could never be angry with you. I owe you my life."

"No, you don't."

"Yes, I do. Truly I do. Meeting me the first day, chasing along beside me to tell me things, warning me about Lord and Lady Stayne. If you hadn't done that, I never would have taken the blanket with me, and Alice and I would both have frozen. You saved us at the start, and Harold Pomfret-Watkin saved us at the end. I wasn't much use at all."

John looked at her. "You truly believe that, don't you?"

"It's true."

"No. The truth is, Laurel Bybank by herself saved Alice Plunderell. That's all there is to it."

"I would have put her in terrible danger with my foolish idea last night, but for Harold Pomfret-Watkin."

"Not so. Shall I tell you something?"

"What?"

"You'll not believe me."

"I know you wouldn't lie to me."

"Harold Pomfret-Watkin came here only because of you, for your sake. He's in the library. He'll tell you himself. He wants to marry you."

"That's foolish."

"Come." He led the way out of the trophy room, and into the library. Inside, Harold Pomfret-Watkin was standing in front of the fireplace with a potato in his hand. He turned and smiled at both of them.

"Ah," he said. "Good. Can someone eat one of these things cold? Will it kick up a typhoon in the innards? Laurel, you know about such things."

"Not everyone thinks so, but I think cold potato is better than warm. It's no more likely to make you ill, I'm sure of that." She looked to her left, to get John's opinion. He was gone.

Harold Pomfret-Watkin brought the potato up close

to his face and examined it, and then he went to the fireplace and dropped it in. "I came because of you. Did John tell you? I meant him to. That's why I won't eat the potato. I don't want anything in my system which has the slightest chance of drawing my attention away from you." He smiled, showing his large front teeth. "Did you sleep well in spite of last night's alarms? Not the best for female sensibilities, that's certain."

Laurel took a short half step back. "I slept very well, thank you."

"Are you ready to tour me around the manor? Get me acquainted?"

"I've not seen it in daylight myself. I don't really know it."

"Then we'll see it together. I thought we might stroll down to the river and look at the house and grounds from there. I see you have your old cloak over your arm, which I find very charming, I must say. Well, shall we go?"

"Before I do anything else, I ought to see if Alice is awake," Laurel said. "Bring her some tea if she wants it."

Harold Pomfret-Watkin shook his head. "That is in no way necessary, not anymore. Servants serve tea, dear Laurel. That's what they're for. Hasn't Alice a cord in her room she can tug if she needs attending? Surely she must."

"I'll go and make sure," Laurel said. "I'll be back shortly." She turned and walked out of the room, across the hall, through the trophy room and into the back hall, where she stopped. It was dim and silent, except for the faraway sounds of the kitchen. She took a deep breath, folded her hands under her chin, closed her eyes, and thought about heaven. After a minute she saw it—the high clouds, the green fields, the faraway mountains where God lived in glory unspeakable, the wide, clean roads, the marble terraces as big as farms. On a balcony overlooking the earth stood her mother, and Father Simpson, and Granny Piersall. Her mother was standing in the middle. She had on a white dress with a narrow skirt and puffy sleeves. Her hair was brushed down her back, and she looked very happy. She raised her right arm and began to wave, and Laurel waved back.

All three of them smiled. They looked very happy. "It's true," Laurel whispered. "I was faithful. I did my duty. Day in, day out, I never thought of giving it up. And I was clever, most of the time. I did my duty and I never thought of saying nay. I prayed, not as often as I should, but there it was. I would have died rather than leave her."

Laurel's mother nodded, and then heaven started to draw back, and then it was gone.

Laurel opened her eyes. Helen was standing next to her, holding a basket of apples. "Are you all right? Not sick, are you?"

"No, I'm fine."

Helen smiled. "That's good. Well, as you can see, I'm still here." She held up a sack. "I just came up from the basement with these. Mrs. Hemmings is going to make apples and Scotch bread. She's afraid to use the oven until it's been cleaned. Might catch fire. You know Mrs. Hemmings? Want to come along to the kitchen with me?"

She turned and went down the hall, and Laurel followed her into the kitchen. Helen put the apple basket on the table, got a small knife, and began to work on them. Mrs. Hemmings was rolling dough at the other end.

"Mrs. Hemmings?" Laurel said. "I thought I might fetch some tea for Lady Alice."

"Helen will bring it up directly."

"I'm here. Nothing easier," Laurel said. "I shouldn't take Helen's time from you."

Mrs. Hemmings put down her rolling pin and started putting a tray together. "If you insist."

"Thank you."

Mrs. Hemmings put her hand up. "It will only take a minute." Laurel stepped back and watched her work.

"Done," Mrs. Hemmings said. "Let it steep a bit before you pour it. I'll send Helen with you."

"No need, thank you."

A minute later Laurel was putting the tea tray on Alice's night table. Alice had rolled over and was facing the wall now. Laurel stood watching her for a minute, and then sat down on the edge of the bed. Alice turned back and opened her eyes and frowned.

"What time is it?"

"After ten."

"Are we all right?"

"They're gone forever."

Alice pulled herself up until her head was propped against the headboard. "Then I won't worry. I heard you when you went out the door this morning. As it was closing, I called, but not very loudly. I only wanted to know where you were going. I worried you were running away, and that woke me up enough to see it was silly. Were you down in the kitchen all this time?"

"I was talking with John and Harold Pomfret-Watkin."

"Why don't you call Harold by his first name? I'm sure he'd like that."

Laurel said nothing.

Alice reached out and took her hand. "I'm more sure than ever of what I told you in the cave. I want to marry John. And you must marry Harold, and make everyone happy."

Laurel got up and went to the stove and began to fix the fire. "I don't want to marry anyone. I can't think of marrying."

"Why ever not? Girls get married at fourteen all the time. Not in our social class, to be sure, but it's done. Do you know the story of the Duchess of Malfi? It's true. Or at least Aunt Salvia said it was. She used to tell it to me to frighten me, but it never really did. The Duchess of Malfi fell madly in love with her steward and proposed to him, begged him even, and though he said no at first, he really did love her and it finally happened. It was paradise for them at the beginning, but then her brother the Bishop found out and everything went smash. Murders, drownings, stranglings, everyone in a rage. That was hundreds of years ago, of course, and it was in a Catholic country. Must you fix the fire right now?"

"No."

"Come sit on my bed. You must tell me again, for the last time, so I know it's not a dream, that you don't want to marry John."

"I don't want to marry John."

"Honor bright?"

"Honor bright."

"Good. Let's drink tea and send for cakes and stuff ourselves until we burst and not see anybody until noon."

16

LAUREL AND ALICE stayed in Alice's room the whole morning drinking tea, eating hot apples and Scotch bread, trying on dresses, and talking about John. Only one dress was long enough for Laurel, an apricot velvet, very pale, that Alice said was the exact color of her hair with the sunlight through it.

At one o'clock Harold Pomfret-Watkin came knocking on the door. "Don't ask me in, Laurel, because I'm not coming in," he said when she opened it. "There's no use in inviting me. One doesn't enter a lady's bedchamber before the maid has been there, and you don't qualify anymore. Ha-ha-ha."

Alice came and stood next to Laurel. "Do you know where John is, by any chance?" she asked.

He shrugged his shoulders. "Seeing after the welfare of everything under the Plunderell sky, wouldn't you think? When you come down, you can search for him." He pointed his finger at Laurel. "And you, dear Laurel, must have a walk with me. Agreed?"

"As soon as I can. But I have a few things I must do first."

Harold Pomfret-Watkin grinned. "I'll be in the front hall. Five minutes?"

"We'll both come down," Alice said, and closed the door slowly. She looked at Laurel. "Find John and talk to him? Please?"

"If Harold Pomfret-Watkin lets me go."

"I'll carry him off somewhere. Just tell John how I care for him. Do you know what you'll say to him? Not that I want you to tell me. I don't. It will all come to you. As long as you don't frighten him, that's the chief thing. And I'll meet you here as soon as I can."

Laurel and Alice combed each other's hair and went downstairs. Harold Pomfret-Watkin was in the library looking at a book of bird pictures. Alice went straight to him and took his arm. "There's something I want you to see in the upstairs hall. I need you to tell me if it's cupids or angels."

"Right this very moment?"

"It can't wait, truly."

Laurel went quickly out the front door and around to the stable. If John wasn't there, she didn't know where he might be, but he was there, sorting out the smithing tools.

"Have you someone to take Mr. Regius's place?" she said.

He shook his head. "There isn't anyone as good. Did Lady Alice get her tea?"

"Yes. Thank you."

"You should have on a cloak, or at least stand where it's warm."

Laurel moved so that she was in the sunlight, and

they looked at each other in silence for a minute. John coughed.

"Are you catching cold?"

He shook his head. "Something in my throat."

"That's good. Mustn't let the steward fall ill."

John coughed again. "There's something I must tell you. Something has happened, and Lady Alice should know about it. It would be best if you told her."

"I have something I should tell you, too," Laurel said.

"What?"

Laurel looked down at the ground, and then looked back at him. "Would you mind very much going first?"

"It's easily told," John said, but then he was silent for a few seconds. "Lord and Lady Stayne are dead. They went out on the river with a lantern. They must have been looking for jewels. They left the wagon and horses at this end of the bridge. The animals were nearly frozen."

Laurel's heart stopped for a moment. "God have mercy on their souls."

John smiled. "Amen."

"Does Mr. Pomfret-Watkin know?"

"It was his notion that I should tell you to tell her."

"Oh."

"He's a very thoughtful man."

"I'm sure."

"Maybe they found a ruby or something and began fighting over it. They would, from time to time. Fight."

"I know." She took a deep breath. "Well, now I should tell you what I have to tell you."

John ran his foot along the edge of a stall and waited. "Yes?"

"Lady Alice would like you to marry her. That's the

long and short of it. If you don't do it, she's bound to be very, very unhappy. She will propose to you, if she must, but it will make her blush. Now you know."

She heard a noise behind her. It was Harold Pomfret-Watkin. "Whispering secrets?"

"No. Speaking them right out loud."

He shrugged. "Not loudly enough. But never mind. Shall we go for our stroll?"

"Not yet. Alice must have a birthday party tonight, and I must get her a present."

Harold Pomfret-Watkin smiled. "Dear, sweet Laurel, she doesn't expect a present from anyone on such short notice. And certainly not from you."

Laurel smiled. "I must."

Harold Pomfret-Watkin looked at John. "Ah, the Female. Too charming for words, don't you think? Laurel, you will always find me prepared to assist. I will happily give you some money ahead, and we will fly into town together and purchase your little birthday geegaw, and on our way I will open my plans to you. Sound tempting?"

Laurel shook her head. "Thank you ever so much, but I have her gift already. I just need to make certain it's where I last saw it. You mustn't come with me. It's a surprise for everyone."

She went around him, and then picked up the front of her skirt and ran across the yard as fast as she could. She went through the kitchen, nodding to Mrs. Hemmings as she passed, into the dining room, where Helen was setting the table with linen and silverware and candlesticks, and up the big staircase and into Lord Stayne's room. It was dark, and cold, and it smelled of dead cigars. Somewhere, there was a mouse scratching.

She looked at Lord Stayne's chair and thought of the time he had made her take out her wallet and empty it onto his lap. "Dead," she whispered. "Never again in this world. God have mercy."

She crossed the room to the high window and pushed aside the curtain. In the sunlight, the room looked larger. She looked at the rug and the dirty bed. A chill ran up her back. She wanted to call in a crew of strong men and clear everything out, carry it all to the middle of a field far away and set fire to it. Then she would scrub the floor, the walls, the ceiling, everything. Maybe then the room could be lived in again.

"If you're here, Lord Stayne, hanging on a few days, I know you can't hurt me. I'm sorry for what happened to you, dying so suddenly, but you brought it on yourself, by not caring for anyone else. Now I am going to take back what is rightfully and properly mine, nothing more."

She walked around the red leather chair to the closet and opened it and looked inside. Directly in the middle, hanging on a velvet hanger, was his red silk dressing gown. The left pocket had a lump in it. She closed her eyes and reached inside and felt her chalks. She lifted them out, blew off the little bits of lint and tobacco, closed her hand on them, and left the room.

To keep from meeting Harold Pomfret-Watkin, she went to the far end of the hall and climbed up to the servants' floor. No one was there. Most of the doors were open, which gave light, and there were cloth bags and satchels and wicker baskets here and there. She stood in front of one room and looked at the chalks to make sure none of them was damaged, and then she went down the back stairs to Alice's room.

Alice was just inside the door, waiting for her. "What kept you?"

"It's a secret. You'll find out tonight at your birthday party."

"Am I having a birthday party?"

"I just decided."

"What did you say to John?"

"That you wanted him to marry you."

"Just like that?"

"That seemed the best thing to do. He didn't have time to say anything back. Harold Pomfret-Watkin broke in on us. The simpler the better. Do you need me now? I'd like to take a walk. There's something I must do."

Alice's eyes suddenly got wider. "You're not going far? You'll be back soon, won't you?"

"Absolutely, I promised apples to some horses. They're not far. I'll be back long before dark."

Alice looked toward the sewing basket. "I could sew while you're gone, I suppose. Mend something? And I'm not alone in the house."

"No. The old servants are coming back. There will be walls and walls of people everywhere. You can hardly keep away from them."

"Do you think I should go and look for John?"

Laurel took her hand. "Whatever you do will be right. There's nothing for you to be afraid of. You're going to have a happy life. I know it."

Alice smiled. "You always make me feel better. Kiss me goodbye? Tell me we're friends?"

"We're friends forever."

They kissed goodbye, and Laurel took her old cloak and went downstairs and out through the kitchen, getting four apples out of the basket on the way. The yard was empty. She entered the stable, said hello to the horses, and went down the corridor to the back, where Mr. Regius's room was. "Her first boy can get the blue one, and her first girl can get the pink one," she said to herself. "Maybe I'll go to America and find some more for the others. She's bound to have at least six."

She came to a heavy door, slid the bolt, and opened it. There was a narrow bed against the wall across from the door, and a small table with a candle on it, and a chair. "I know you won't mind this," she said. In the corner was a small wooden trunk. She opened it up, and on the top shelf, wrapped in tissue paper, were five handkerchiefs. They were all a little yellow, but none was mended or patched. Laurel chose the top one, which had a blue line embroidered around it. She closed the trunk, put the chalks in the handkerchief, put it in her pocket with the apples, and left the stable, going out through the rear gate and around the outside of the garden to the road, so that Harold Pomfret-Watkin wouldn't see her.

She didn't see the hole Lord and Lady Stayne had made in the ice until she was on the bridge, and then it was the sunlight on the brass lantern lying next to it that first caught her attention. She went over to the chain rail and stood looking down. She knew what it was like to slide toward the water in daylight and almost go in. What must it have been like to drop suddenly in the dark? "Lord, have mercy upon their souls," she said, and crossed herself. Then she hurried on.

She walked very fast, and after a few minutes she was sweating. She undid the top buttons of her cloak, and a minute later took it off. She looked down. She liked the way the bottom of her brown dress looked, brushing the snow. "Dear God," she said, "I know it's a tiny thing set next to the prayers of the sick and dying and poor, but please let those horses be there. I'm grateful for everything Thou hast done to preserve my life, and Thy will be done, but I did promise them apples ever so long ago. Well, it seems long. In the name of the Father and the Son and the Holy Ghost. Amen."

She held her cloak up in front of her and reached into the pocket to make sure the apples hadn't fallen out, and then she thought about Alice's wedding, how Alice and John would look saying their vows, and dancing at the party afterward. It would be an afternoon wedding, and an evening party, and she would wear the apricot dress and dance as long as the music went on.

She came to the field. The horses were there, standing a little way back from the fence. She stopped by some trees. "Thank you, dear Jesus." She put her cloak back on so that her hands would be free, took out the biggest apple, and started walking again, slowly, holding it out so the horses could see it.

They looked at her.

"Good day. Remember, I promised you apples? Don't bolt now. You know me. I'm a friend."

She reached the fence and stepped up onto a flat stone, holding the apple out on the palm of her hand.

The bigger horse eyed it a minute and then came over, a few short steps at a time, throwing his head first to the left and then to the right. When he was so close that she could see the small scars on his face, he stretched out his neck and sucked the apple in.

"Now we must feed your friend," Laurel said, and threw two apples in front of the smaller horse. Then she took out the last apple. "I should have brought more. One for myself, come to that. Next time I'll bring seven. Of course, you mustn't have too many on your winter stomachs."

She looked back along the road and saw Harold Pomfret-Watkin coming toward her. She stepped down off her stone and waited for him.

He stopped a few steps away. "Here you are, my skittery little fawn. I was ready to walk all the way to Saltfield. May I lend you company for the way back to Plunderell Manor?"

"Thank you."

"You need to be a bit more prudent. It isn't good for a female to be out on the road alone. And when she has become a young woman of means, it's quite impossible."

"I would have been back before dark."

He smiled a quick smile. "Nevertheless, it's not wise for a female to form the habit of adventure. Are those animals friends of yours?"

"I came to give them some apples."

"Shall I purchase them for you?"

"No, thank you. I don't even know if they're for sale."

"Oh, you can be sure they are. It's simply a matter of discovering the price. You could stable them at the manor. Or with me in Hampshire. We always have room. Or we can add some, if you really fancy having them. Say the word."

"No, truly, thank you. I don't want to own them."

He smiled. "Perhaps Alice owns them. This could still be manor land. She'd gladly make you a present of them."

"I like them belonging to someone else," she said, looking back at them.

"You're very quaint, Laurel Bybank, if that's the word I want. I hope to court you. Quite seriously. If you had parents, I'd be in front of them this very moment asking their permission to call on you."

"I'm too young to be courted. Besides, I'm going to America."

Harold Pomfret-Watkin slapped his chest with his hand. "I have infinite patience. I have a cousin. Have I mentioned her? Barbara? Likely not. At her last birthday she was sixteen, and she was already promised to a young man, informally of course, four years ago, when she was only twelve. So there you are, aren't you? She goes to a wonderful school. You could go there with her. I don't know exactly what they teach. Useful and pleasant things, I'm sure. She seems to enjoy it. And on holidays my mother and I could come down and visit with you for an afternoon, or you could come stay with us."

"Have you any friends in America?"

"No. I have a third cousin in Boston. But, truth to tell, we've never met. We could change that, of course. Voyages, they say, are very pleasant. Shall I go with you? Get some sea air. We'd be suitably chaperoned, of course. It would be absolutely proper. Are you listening? I'm the one talking, not the horses."

She turned and looked at him. "I'm sorry. I was listening carefully."

"Not to put too fine a point on it, Laurel, I was proposing marriage. Not now, but later. Sometime, you will need to marry. All your other prospects depend on it. A married woman can do what she wants. Learn to play the piano. You have beautiful hands, you know, by the grace of the angels not yet ruined. Study drawing, if she has an interest. Be hostess at marvelous parties. Take French lessons. I haven't even mentioned travel. And, of course, there are children."

Laurel took a deep breath. "Mr. Pomfret-Watkin, I want to walk home, and I don't want to talk anymore."

"Oh? Absolutely." He put his hand to his mouth. "My lips are buttoned. Are you watching me button them? My silence will show you what a strong character I have. See how I do it?"

Laurel put her finger to her lips. "Shhhhhh . . ."

17

LAUREL AND HAROLD POMFRET-WATKIN walked all the way from the horse field to the manor without saying a word. John and Alice came to meet them at the bridge.

"We have something to tell you," John said. "We are engaged to be married."

Alice took his arm. "It won't be a long engagement, but our marriage ceremony won't be hasty, either."

Harold Pomfret-Watkin clapped his hands. "Just the thing. Absolutely the exact thing. Who cares what anyone else thinks?"

Laurel took Alice's hand and kissed it. Now she had truly come home, and was safe. "I must run ahead," she said, "or else I'll start dancing."

That night, at Alice's birthday party, John wore a formal suit that had once belonged to Alice's grandfather, and stood up and made a speech praising Laurel for saving Alice's life. Then he and Alice together gave her the biggest diamond from the treasure chest, which she immediately gave to Harold Pomfret-Watkin for safekeeping. She wasn't absolutely sure it would be safe with him, but she knew if he lost it he would go out and get her another.

They went to their rooms at midnight, and Alice insisted that Laurel sleep with her in her bed. "It's bigger than that one we slept in with that farm girl. What was her name?"

"Eleanor."

"Yes. Eleanor. It's bigger than that bed, and there are only two of us, and we're both very thin now. Too thin. We have to get a little fatter. Don't you think?"

"Yes, I think we should. Alice? I have something for you. An engagement present more than a birthday one."

She handed Alice the handkerchief with the chalks inside. "They're for your children. They're very rare, especially the blue one. Most blue ones are much paler. I found them myself."

Alice took the chalks and looked at them, started to cry, and embraced Laurel, and Laurel started to cry, and it was a long time before their eyes were dry and they were in bed under the covers.

"You'll love Egypt," Alice said. "That's where we're going on our honeymoon. My parents' graves are there."

Laurel looked at Alice for a few moments in silence. "I won't go on your honeymoon, Alice. Not even the closest of friends do that."

"Not in the same room. I know that. But you can be down the hall."

"No. I'm going to America. Not forever. I'll come back in lots of time to play with your first baby. You won't miss me."

"Promise?"

"Absolutely."

Alice wiggled down under the covers. "I will, too, miss you," she said. After a while she let go of Laurel's hand and fell asleep. Laurel stayed awake, thinking of Boston, and how it would be living in a foreign city alone. "It's the same heaven up above no matter where you are," she said to herself, and closed her eyes. As she started to drift asleep she saw her mother, and Father Simpson, and Granny Piersall, waving to her from their balcony. She lifted her fingers and waved back.